Dancing With a Royal

THE UNEXPECTED ROYALS
BOOK ONE

TOMI TABB

All rights reserved. No part of this publication may be reproduced, stored or transmitted in any form or by any means, electronic, mechanical, photocopying, recording, scanning, or otherwise without written permission from the publisher. It is illegal to copy this book, post it to a website, or distribute it by any other means without permission. This book may also not be used for any AI training purposes.

This novel is entirely a work of fiction. The names, characters and incidents portrayed in it are the work of the author's imagination. Any resemblance to actual persons, living or dead, events or localities is entirely coincidental.

Designations used by companies to distinguish their products are often claimed as trademarks. All brand names and product names used in this book and on its cover are trade names, service marks, trademarks and registered trademarks of their respective owners. The publishers and the book are not associated with any product or vendor mentioned in this book. None of the companies referenced within the book have endorsed the book.

First edition

First published by Pas de Chat Publications 2020 Copyright © 2020 by Tomi Tabb

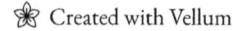

❦ Created with Vellum

To my sister

Prologue

ONE YEAR AGO

"Has anyone seen Clara?" the stage manager of the Los Angeles Ballet Theatre shouted frantically.

Dancers adorned in costumes from the Land of the Sweets jumped up and down on the stage, warming up before the start of the second act, while the orchestra tuned their instruments, and technicians inspected the ground closely for any stray fake snowflakes.

"Clara Little, where are you?"

"There was a problem with her pointe shoe," a dancer in an orange tutu offered. "The shank snapped. She went to grab her backup shoes. She should be back any minute."

The stage manager frowned. "Well, can you go and find her? Lily just went down. I need her to dance the Sugar Plum variation."

A backdrop was slowly being lowered from the ceiling as the sleigh carrying the character Clara and her

Nutcracker Prince was positioned into the upper left corner of the stage.

"Five minutes people. Five minutes 'til Act II."

"Did someone call my name?" Clara walked over, fanning herself. She'd only been gone for three minutes.

"Finally!" Placing her hand on Clara's forearm, the stage manager tugged her to the side of the stage. "Lily's out. You're in. You have three minutes to change into her tutu."

Clara's eyes widened. "What? Is she okay?"

"She'll live. Sprained ankle." The stage manager pulled the ivory, soft-pink, and gold costume off a rolling rack and shoved it into her arms. "You two have roughly the same torso size, so this should do. If it's too loose or too tight, you're just going to have to roll with it."

"And I'm dancing Sugar Plum?"

"Yes," the stage manager said. "Three minutes, people! This is your three-minute warning!"

Clara yelped and leapt behind the quick-change screen. The rough tulle scratched her skin. There was no time to dwell on the fact that this was the big opportunity she'd longed for. She was at last stepping into a role outside the corps deballet.

Clara was a quick study when it came to learning choreography. The LABT used her often as an understudy, but normally, she never debuted the parts she learned. She was the company's backup to the backup. At times, she wondered if Artum, the company's artistic director, even saw her as being more than just a corps dancer.

Her pulse rate increased. Her palms grew sweaty. "Who's my prince tonight? I didn't have a chance to read over the call sheets."

"It's Louis," the stage manager replied.

Clara breathed a small sigh of relief. Louis was an excellent partner. She'd danced with him as a guest of the Fresno Community Ballet last year.

She stepped out from behind the screen.

"We don't have time to mess with the tiara, but here's your wand. Merde."

The dancers cleared the stage. The crowd clapped. The orchestra began playing the overture for Act II.

All my hard work in the studio comes down to ten minutes of dancing.

She wondered if Lily's injury meant she might be asked to dance the remainder of her shows. As a corps de ballet member, Clara performed every night in both the first and second act of *The Nutcracker*. It was a punishing schedule that pushed the corps dancers to the breaking point every holiday season. Soloists and principals, however, had the luxury of only dancing every few days, and only for short periods of time.

At twenty-five, her body didn't recover as quickly as it did when she was twenty. A day off here or there would do wonders for her body, mind, and spirit.

I can't get too far ahead of myself. Focus on the present.

The curtain rose and Clara entered the stage.

∼

The red velvet curtain closed for the last time. Clara gently placed the five bouquets of flowers onto the ground and hugged the sweaty Louis.

"Little, you nailed it! I mean, I knew you would," he exclaimed.

"The look in your eyes when you saw me enter the stage instead of Lily was priceless." Clara laughed, releasing a deep sigh of relief. "Tonight was definitely a trial by fire."

As they let go, Artum and a man in a charcoal-gray crewneck sweater approached the pair. Louis excused himself.

"Clara Little! You were stunning. Simply stunning. I was telling Artum how lucky he is to have a dancer with such musicality on his staff. If he's not careful, another company might just lure you away." The man in the sweater grinned widely. "I'm Igor Radovsky, director of the Monte Carlo Royal Ballet and the World Stars of Ballet tour group." He extended his hand to her.

Her cheeks burned as she shook it. "Igor, it's an honor."

"I hope I'll be able to watch you dance once more before I leave LA."

He and Clara both glanced at Artum. He was a balding man with raven-black hair, a beard, and glasses.

"You did well tonight, Clara. Igor's been singing your praises nonstop. You've made *quite* an impression," Artum commended. His steel eyes appraised her as if he'd discovered a luxury car that fit into his budget. "I was thinking that since we have no way of knowing how long Lily may be out, I could count on you to dance the rest of her scheduled performances."

Clara bobbed her head up and down. "Yes, sir. Of course."

"Good." His lips curved. "If you're as well received the rest of the season as you were tonight, you just may find yourself being promoted."

Her heart swelled. Those were the words she'd longed to hear.

Igor's eyes danced with excitement. "You're a future star in the making. I wonder if I might be able to convince you to guest in the gala performances I'm staging in New York and Washington DC, this spring, with Louie Gascon as your partner."

"Of course she will," Artum answered on her behalf.

"Then that settles it." Igor clapped his hands together. "I'll give Artum the details to pass on to you later. Doubtless you have plans to celebrate your performance tonight. It was nice meeting you."

Igor and Artum offered her a few more well wishes, then moved on to speaking with some of the other dancers.

Clara's head spun. Solo roles? Guesting? It was all too much to wrap her mind around. She'd always struggled to stand out from the crowd, and now, it was finally her turn. She'd arrived.

Chapter One
CLARA

For the past three days, Clara had lived, breathed, and dreamed about the wedding pas de deux from the classical ballet *The Sleeping Beauty*.

She pinched her forearm, still not believing that she, little old Clara, had been asked to replace the Bolshoi Ballet's prima ballerina, Maria Tsukyskia, in the World Stars of Ballet gala as a last-minute fill in. In the ballet world, everybody knew Maria's name.

"Nope, you're not dreaming, you are heading to London, C," her best friend Amanda said, glancing over to her from the driver's seat.

"You're sure?"

"Positive. Now finish your coffee. I promise, it'll sink in once you're more awake."

Clara reached for the still half-filled coffee and took a large sip. The thrill of going on this trip almost matched the adrenaline rush she received every time she stepped onto a stage.

I've spent four years in the corps de ballet biding my time to become a soloist. And now, only a week after my promotion finally came through, I'm about to give one of the biggest performances of my life. I guess what they say is true... when it rains, it pours.

Amanda exited the freeway and drove up the ramp to the passenger drop-off area of Los Angeles International Airport. An airplane's engines roared overhead. Cars and transit vans boldly darted across lanes of traffic without warning, but Clara never worried. She knew she was in good hands with Amanda. Even if her bestie's driving scared her to death half the time.

Clara replaced the coffee cup in the drink holder just as the car jerked to the right. The brakes emitted a high-pitched squeak. She gripped on to the armrest tightly, and her fingers turned white. She smelled burning rubber.

I spoke too soon.

"Sorry, I forgot that if I don't drop you here, I'll have to double back onto the freeway to reach the employee lot. There's *always* construction going on at LAX."

Clara's heart rate was slowly returning to normal. "No biggie." She opened the car door. "Thanks for the ride, A."

"Anytime, C. Anytime." Amanda tapped the hazard-lights button, then popped the trunk. They rounded the back of the car, and she helped Clara pull out her garment bag and rolling suitcase. "Remember, you've got this. Never doubt yourself. They invited you to the gala for a reason." Amanda wrapped her arms around Clara's petite frame and squeezed tightly.

"I will. I promise."

"Great." Amanda released her. "Then all that's left is for me to tell you to have a safe flight. Text me if you get bored waiting at the gate."

Clara collected her rolling luggage and jogged from the island to the terminal. Turning around, she waved

DANCING WITH A ROYAL

and watched Amanda hop back into the car and speed off.

Entering the terminal, Clara plopped her belongings down on a section of hard plastic chairs and reshuffled everything.

Makeup and liquids are in here. Costume in there. Pointe shoes in my tote. Everything else is in the rolling bag. I think I'm good to go.

She headed over to the teal self-service ticket kiosks for Pacific Skyways. The caffeine from the caramel macchiato she'd downed was beginning to kick in and gave her the extra jolt of energy she needed to be a fully functioning member of society.

Clara tapped the check-in button on the kiosk monitor, following the instructions to verify her reservation information on the machine. Just as she scanned the photo page of her passport, the screen flashed an angry red error message, prompting her to try again.

That's weird. Maybe I just had it angled wrong.

Placing her tote bag on the ground, she attempted to scan the document once more. Frustratingly, she received the same error message.

She huffed, and the muscles in her neck tensed. *I hate technology.* She released a deep breath. *It's fine. This is why I wanted to arrive early—in case I had problems. The ticket agent can fix whatever is going on here. I just have to stay calm. There isn't a reason for me to get upset.*

She walked over to the ticket counter queue. A set of five bored-looking airline agents stood chatting about their weekend. She stood by the stanchions waiting, tapping her hand against her thigh and mentally reviewing the choreography of *The Sleeping Beauty.*

Finally, a full minute later, the agents noticed a line

forming. Swiftly, they fled to their various stations and signaled the waiting passengers over to them.

"Next!"

Clara rushed over to a yawning man with a bald spot.

"Hi, I'm here for Flight 769 direct to London Heathrow. The kiosk wouldn't let me finish checking in for some reason."

"May I see your passport, please?" he asked.

She handed it over. He opened the item and verified her information against the computer. Satisfied, the agent clicked through a few screens, and let out a low whistle. "Oh, 769."

"Yes?" The muscles in her stomach tightened.

The agent's brow furrowed. "Uh… it looks like that flight has been delayed five hours. Mechanical issues with the plane. Your new scheduled departure time is one p.m."

She gulped and did the mental math. With the time change, this would put her in London at nine a.m. She needed to be checked in to the hotel and ready for rehearsal for the gala performance by three p.m.

"I have to get to London as soon as possible. Are there any other flights I can take that would get me in around the same time as the original flight? Or maybe you could reroute me through another city, like Paris or Amsterdam?"

Clara gripped the handle of her travel purse hard. Anxiety crept up as she began to fear more things might go wrong. What if the flight ended up being canceled? What if she lost her only chance to rehearse before the show?

No. She had to stay optimistic.

Everything happens for a reason. Just like Maria having to pull out. I'm meant to be there.

Despite the circumstances being beyond her control,

she remained determined to adapt and make the most of whatever came her way.

The clerk shook his head. "Flight 769 to London Heathrow is completely full. Last night's red-eye was canceled. But"—he stared at Clara with a blank expression—"if you wanted to volunteer to take a later flight, I can upgrade you to first class."

Hadn't he listened at all to what she'd said earlier? Her cheeks flushed. "No. I'm on a tight deadline."

The clerk held his hands up. "I'm sorry. I'm just doing my job." He cleared his throat. "Are you planning to check your bag in today?"

She sighed and reluctantly glanced over to her rolling bag, knowing it would likely have to be checked anyway, especially if it was a full flight. "I guess." She double-checked one more time that she had her costume, pointe shoes, and other key items in her carry-on, then placed the bag on the scale.

"Thanks. You can pick it up in London. Here are your boarding pass and claim ticket. Your seat will be assigned at the gate. Is there anything else I can help you with today?"

"Where can I find the strongest cup of coffee in the terminal?"

"Norma's Café, across from the book stand."

"Thanks."

~

Clara's eyes fluttered as she sniffed the air. There was nothing better than the smell of roasting coffee beans.

I'm gonna treat myself to something special. Do I want a piece of pumpkin bread or a cinnamon twist to go with my vanilla latte? Hmm. Choices. Choices.

She stood on her toes to have a better look in the display case.

Oh, they have fresh banana muffins too. Gah. Should I just buy one of everything?

Her phone chimed. She pulled the device from her handbag's outer pocket and unlocked the screen.

Amanda: Just finished our debrief. I have two minutes to spare before we start boarding the plane. Are you all checked in?

Clara hesitated. Should she fill her bestie in? No. Amanda didn't need to be burdened with her problems when she was about to work a twelve-hour flight.

Clara: Yes.

She snapped a photo of the café.

Clara: Just waiting for coffee and deciding on pastries.

Amanda: Another coffee? Get the pumpkin bread. I know it's your favorite.

Clara: I love my caffeine.

Amanda: *face-palm emoji*

Clara: *cheesy grin emoji*

Three dots blinked. Amanda was typing.

Clara: I meant to ask you earlier, but where *are* you heading today?

Amanda: Zurich! And before you ask, yes, I'll pick up a couple boxes of Swiss chocolates!

She fist pumped.

Clara: I heart you.

Amanda: I'm the bestie for a reason… Gotta run. My purser is yelling at me to put my phone away.

Clara: Text me when you land. Have a good flight.

Amanda: Same to you.

It doesn't seem that long ago that I was student at the

Seattle Ballet Academy and Amanda a flight attendant trainee at the Pacific Skyways Headquarters.

Memories of late-night study sessions flooded her mind, where she'd quiz Amanda about what she'd learned that day. Those sessions had transformed Clara into someone almost fluent in aviation speak. Terms like *push back* and *pax* might mean nothing to the average person; however, to Clara, they meant *departure from the gate* and *passengers*.

Reaching the front of the coffee queue, she changed tactics and made the executive decision to switch her order to a green tea latte. She needed something soothing that would last a little longer than her coffee. She still had a ten-and-a-half-hour flight ahead of her.

~

Latte in hand, Clara strolled past the high-end shops in the terminal at a leisurely pace, studying the people around her. Airports brought together people from every walk of life. Watching them and trying to piece together their stories was better than any form of entertainment, except for maybe dance.

Families hurried by, adorned in Disney-themed attire. Businessmen clad in suits navigated the terminal, juggling phone calls and searching for a charging spot for their laptops.

Securing her own quiet spot, Clara sat down. However, just as she pulled out her copy of *National Geographic* and flipped to the first article, a sinking feeling took hold in her stomach—she'd left her pumpkin bread at the café. She groaned.

If she went back, what were the chances it would still be

there? Did she even want to walk all the way back down the terminal?

I did spend six bucks on it. It's not like it's even that far. I'm just being lazy.

Jumping to her feet, she trekked back to the café. Approaching the barista, she asked, "Um, excuse me. Did you happen to see a pumpkin loaf sitting around here?"

The barista, occupied with calling out drink orders behind the counter, shook her head and shrugged. "Sorry. No idea."

Clara's shoulders slumped. "Okay. Thanks anyway."

Walking away from the café, she considered her next move. She still had four and a half hours of time to kill. If she didn't eat now, she'd be starving in the next hour. On an average day, she ate a big snack between her ten and eleven a.m. rehearsals to tide her over until lunch at one.

Earlier, I ordered the last piece of pumpkin bread. The case was still empty when I walked past. So I guess the universe is trying to tell me to eat a real lunch.

Making her way to the nearest newsstand and snack shop, Clara contemplated whether she should splurge on a ten-dollar ham sandwich or go for the fifteen-dollar chicken club. She bent her knees and picked up one of each, weighing them in her hand. Neither looked particularly appealing.

"I guess the chicken is the winner," she said to herself.

She returned the ham to the cooler and picked up a few other snacks. As she turned, a tall man with sandy-blond hair caught her attention. He was impeccably dressed in a navy wool overcoat and tortoiseshell glasses.

He was absorbed by his phone, hardly glancing up as he moved past Clara and haphazardly grabbed his own array of snacks—three peanut butter and jelly cupcakes, a fruit cup, the ham sandwich, and bacon and cheese sliders.

They both joined the line.

"Next!"

The sandy-haired man slid his purchases to the cashier. He shuffled the phone from his left ear to his right. A hint of pink appeared on his cheeks as he fumbled with his pockets, searching for his wallet.

After a moment of struggling, he finally said, "I'll ring you right back," in a posh British accent, and placed his phone on the counter.

I could listen to someone with a voice like yours all day.

On the sidelines, two men exchanged hushed remarks and stifled laughter as they watched the unfolding scene. Clara frowned, puzzled by the situation. If they were his friends or coworkers, why didn't they step in to assist him? Did they find enjoyment in watching him struggle?

"Sir, would you mind stepping to the side so I can take the next customer?" the annoyed clerk asked.

"It was right here. I'm certain of it."

She rolled her eyes. *Men.*

Pulling out her credit card, she asked, "How much does he owe?"

"Thirty-eight dollars even."

The man's phone rang, immediately stealing his attention. Clara doubted he even noticed her.

"Hello? Yes… Eddie called his morning." He pinched the bridge of his nose. "Yes, I'm handling it like I always do…"

She slid her lunch toward the clerk. "Can you add this to the tab, please?"

"Your total is sixty-two dollars and ten cents."

She winced and swiped her credit card against the reader.

I offered. Too late to take it back now.

"I do *not* baby him. Give me one second." Holding the phone to his ear with his shoulder, he muttered a hasty, "Thanks," and scooped up his provisions. "If it were up to me, I'd freeze his access to his bank accounts. Without any money, he's less inclined to do something foolish."

The two men standing off to the side rushed after him toward the gates without a backward glance.

I'll say it again—men! She shook her head.

Clara glanced down at how she was dressed. She wore her favorite pair of black leggings, a comfortable, old black-and-white polka-dotted top, and gray Converse. Her long, dark brown hair was swept up into a messy bun. Like most ballerinas, to the average person, she appeared much younger than her twenty-six years of age.

~

An hour and a half before boarding, right as Clara finished the last article in her magazine about the discovery of new ancient Greek temple ruins on the island of Crete, she heard her name being announced over the PA system near the departure gate.

"Ms. Clara Little, please see the agent at gate number eight for an important message. Again, Ms. Clara Little, please proceed to gate number eight for an important message."

She glanced at her watch, puzzled why Pacific Skyways could possibly be paging her so early. She stood from her seat, stretched, and gathered her belongings.

Every seat in the waiting area was occupied by frustrated and grumpy-looking passengers. She heard the hushed buzz of two hundred or so conversations, and occasionally, the odd crying baby.

"Hi, I'm Clara Little. You paged me?"

"Can I see your ID, please?" The gate agent's voice held a touch of strain. Clara handed over her passport, and after a brief inspection, he returned it to her. "Thanks."

His shoulders were noticeably tense, and a thin sheen of perspiration glistened on his forehead. He stared at his computer screen as he spoke, refusing to meet her eyes, "I'm so sorry, but I have some bad news for you. Flight 769 has been overbooked, and unfortunately, there aren't enough business class seats available for everybody on board. You're one of the passengers who have been moved into the economy class cabin. We apologize for the inconvenience."

She swallowed hard, absorbing the latest piece of bad news. "I mean, I understand, but is there a reason I'm the one getting bumped?"

"Again, we're sorry. Your reservation happened to be one of the last bookings made for business class," the agent explained, a hint of regret in his voice. "We've had to relocate five other business-class passengers and almost all of the passengers booked into the first-class cabin," the agent explained.

"The flight is already arriving late, and now you mean to tell me that my full-fare, two-thousand-dollar business-class ticket is being downgraded to economy?" Even if the gala organizers had been the ones to pay for her ticket, this wasn't right. She placed her hands on her hips. "I don't mean to be rude, but as a full-fare customer, doesn't that entitle me to be accommodated in the business cabin over the people with discounted or reward tickets?"

The "remain calm" mantra Clara usually practiced

wasn't going to work in a situation like this. If she was going to dance coming straight off the plane, she needed that lay-flat business-class seat. It was crucial that she was able to get some sleep and stretch out her legs.

"No, unless you want to take a later flight. We have other passengers on a full-fare basis in the same situation as you. Management tells us what to do. My hands are tied. The best I can do is give you a voucher to pick up a meal from one of the restaurants in the terminal since we won't have the business-class meals available for you. It's good for a value of fifteen dollars. Here's the number for the passenger service line. They'll be able to assist with refunding you the difference in fare. I'm sorry." The agent mopped his forehead and took a step back from the counter.

"Fine. What's my new seat assignment?" Clara's voice was flat, devoid of emotion. The agent handed her the new ticket. "Thanks."

Shifting her purse from one shoulder to the other, she passed by another disgruntled passenger venting their frustrations in the open.

"Get me your manager or someone higher up! I need a competent person who can answer my questions. Not a person who only repeats the garbage excuses they're fed by the airline."

They're right, this is such BS.

She found the first unoccupied chair and sank into it, the feeling of exasperation consuming her. All she wanted to do was sleep and wake up in London, ready to dance. Now she was going to have to get up every hour or two just to keep her body from cramping too badly. Economy seats were *tiny*. Not to mention that fifteen dollars wasn't going

DANCING WITH A ROYAL

to even buy her a decent meal. Just another sandwich and maybe a bottle of water. Today was *not* at all going her way.

She wondered if Amanda was in flight and able to access the on-board Wi-Fi so she could text her. Her bestie was always good for some gossip and helping to take her mind off her problems.

Clara: You there?

Amanda: Always. What's up?

Clara: You won't believe what just happened.

Amanda: Que paso?

Clara: I just got downgraded from business to economy.

Amanda: Ouch. That doesn't happen often. I'm sorry.

Clara: The agents are saying the flight is "oversold," but I find that hard to believe.

Amanda: What are you flying? B-777? B-787? A-220?

Clara: My ticket says 773.

Amanda: It's a Boeing 777-300. One of the newer planes in the fleet. It should hold about 380 people.

Clara: If that's true, then how are all the first-class tickets gone? You're always telling me how empty the first-class cabin is. Wouldn't they usually upgrade business-class passengers to first?

Amanda: That *is* strange.

Clara: The only thing I can think of is that when I checked in, they said one of yesterday's flight was canceled. But still.

Amanda: No, you're definitely right. Even with a cancellation, it would be really weird to downgrade business passengers to *economy*. What was your flight number again?

Clara: I'm on 769 to London.

Amanda: Hold please. One of my friends, Becky, is working on 769 tonight.

Clara waited a few minutes until a ding went off, indicating a text message.

Amanda: Shut the front door. You have a VVIP on your flight.

She stared blankly at the screen. That was one acronym that meant nothing to her.

Clara: What's a VVIP?

Amanda: VVIP means celebrity, royalty, or millionaire. I'm dying to know who it is! Becky just confirmed the VVIP bought out the entire first cabin.

Clara: Let's go with millionaire, since first-class tickets don't come cheap.

Amanda: That's what I'd guess too. Let me know if it's anyone you know (which I doubt).

Clara didn't do social media or have time to keep up with celebrity gossip like Amanda. Her days were filled with endless classes, rehearsals, and performances.

Clara: *Thumbs-up emoji*

Amanda: Text you later. We're about to start the meal service. Good luck and try to remember to leave me tickets with amazing seats at will call. This girl is going straight from the Zurich plane to a plane bound for London to see you tonight.

Clara: Got it! Nosebleed seats, it is!

Amanda: Very funny.

Chapter Two

CLARA

At noon, a voice overhead announced, "Attention, all passengers heading to London Heathrow on Pacific SkywaysFlight 769. We are ready to begin the boarding process. We ask that you please have your boarding pass and passport out and available, ready to be scanned by the gate agent. We kindly ask you to remain seated until your zone is called."

Clara watched as ninety percent of the passengers around her rushed to line up to try to be the first to board when it was the economy cabin's turn. Her bag was checked, so she didn't need to fight for overhead bin space. Her tutu would fit nicely on top of whatever bags were already there.

She spotted the British man from earlier lurking at the front boarding lane, still glued to his phone. Where had he come from? She could swear he hadn't been near the gate when she scanned the area less than two minutes ago.

How had he been able to bypass everyone else lined up in the business-class line? Was he one of those elite Pacific Skyways frequent flyers? The pair of suits traveling with him were more stoic than earlier and kept nervously glancing around them. Maybe they were as frustrated by the delay as the rest of the passengers.

"Sir, if you'll follow me, please." A member of the airline staff guided the man forward.

Another gate agent tapped the gate microphone. A high-pitched static rang out. Clara's hands flew to her ears. "Thank you for your patience. At this time, we'd like to welcome all those passengers seated in our business-class cabin and our Platinum Elite frequent flyers. Welcome aboard."

She pulled out her earbuds and e-reader, so they were within easy reach.

"Next, we'd like to welcome any families traveling with children under the age of two and those individuals who might need a little extra time."

A few families with strollers and little kids walked up to the gate.

"We'd now like to welcome all remaining passengers with ticketed and confirmed seats on Pacific Skyways Flight 769 to London Heathrow to board at this time."

Clara waited for the line to clear and then leisurely walked up to the now empty gate area.

As she held out her board pass to be scanned, the gate agent remarked, "Lucky you, an exit row."

Her eyes widened. "An exit row? Huh, finally something good."

Once on the plane, she settled into her seat. It was conveniently located right off the boarding door, next to the window. Although the flight attendants would sit right across from her in the jump seat as the plane took off and landed, when they weren't there, she would be rewarded with that coveted extra legroom.

Closing her eyes, she allowed her body to relax, and fell asleep.

A short while later, the captain's disembodied voice startled her awake. "Flight attendants, prepare for departure."

She sat taller and rubbed her eyes. Two women in teal airline uniforms found their way to the temporary seats.

"Stinks for all the Z- and J-class pax who had to be moved, but it *is* nice that Leeds is on board," one of them said. "He's always super sweet. I could listen to that man talk all day. His accent is so dreamy."

"When was the last time we flew royalty?"

"A month ago? We had Princess Leonora on board. It happens more often than you'd think."

"I wonder what Paula would say if I snuck up front to deliver some extra hot towels to first."

"Good luck with that. She watches her cabin like a hawk. When we had—"

The sounds of the engines roaring to life killed the rest of the conversation. Clara processed the information she had just heard. The VVIP must be whoever Leeds was. As she had learned from Amanda, Z class was code for first class, and J stood for business class.

Clara's mind went through multiple options and scenarios as she considered if it was worth trying to satisfy her curiosity by sneaking into first class herself.

Except the VVIP probably has an army of security officers. I wonder if they got a private car to take him to the plane, or if he might've passed through the passenger area. If he did, what does he look like?

Ten hours later, the plane landed with no problems and taxied to the gate. Flight 769 had made up time in the air, but it was still four and a half hours later than originally scheduled.

"On behalf of this LA-based cabin crew, thank you for flying Pacific Skyways. Welcome to London," a flight attendant said.

"I made it!" Clara exclaimed.

Landside once more, she stopped at the first restroom she spotted, then followed the signs to passport control and immigration, eventually ending up in baggage claim.

Finding a quiet corner, Clara used the back of a metal chair to go through a basic ballet barre of plies in first through fifth positions and stretch as she waited for the barrage carousel to roar to life. She needed her body in top form.

Ten minutes passed. Twenty minutes passed. Then thirty minutes. One by one, the passengers from her flight collected their luggage, until she was alone.

"Excuse me, do you happen to know if there are any more bags being brought up from this flight?" Clara asked an attendant. "It's been over half an hour."

The elderly woman in a neon safety vest regarded her with a look of sympathy. "Once the belt stops moving, that's it for the flight. Go check with the luggage office. If it's not in there, you can file a claim with the airline. I'll be happy to show you where to go if you need it."

The attendant was a welcome change from the airport workers she had encountered at LAX. Clara sighed and nodded. She followed along at a slower pace, dejected.

"Cheer up, love, things will get better. You just need a nice spot of tea once you get settled," the attendant offered.

"Thank you. I've had a horrible start to my trip," she said with a hint of fatigue.

The woman made sure Clara was settled before heading back to her post near the baggage belt.

Tracing revealed her checked bag was probably still sitting somewhere at LAX.

"We sincerely apologize for the inconvenience. I'll go ahead and flag the case for special handling. As soon as your trolley arrives at Heathrow, we'll have it couriered over to your hotel. Please leave your details here." Clara picked up a pen and copied the name and address of her hotel onto the form.

The luggage office attendant made a few notes on his computer. "The airline is prepared to offer you a voucher good for up to one hundred pounds to assist with purchasing whatever personal items or clothing you need until it arrives. Are you heading to a hotel straightaway? We can also cover your taxi expense."

"Thanks. I would really appreciate the cab fare. I'm feeling little jet-lagged right now and not thinking straight. Can you possibly give me an estimate on how long it might take my bag to reach me?" She stifled a yawn with her hand.

The attendant completed the lost-luggage report for Clara. He gave her a grim smile. "Certainly. The next flight from LAX to LHR is scheduled for tomorrow. At most, it should take up to two days for your bag to reach you."

She tucked a printed copy of the report into her handbag and made a beeline for the taxi stand outside the airport.

The skies were gloomy, but a welcome change from Southern California's blue skies. A light mist came down and reminded Clara of Seattle. She smiled and took in the sound of British accents around her and her first glance at cars being driven on the opposite side of the road.

The taxi stand had a short queue of people ahead of

her, a welcome sight compared to the congestion inside the arrivals area. Several bright flashes going off at the end of the terminal caught her eye. She squinted, trying to make out what was going on. A few tourists rushed from behind her, heading toward the commotion at full speed.

What on earth? It sounds like they're shouting "Leeds." Is that the same person from the plane? She let out another yawn and stretched, lifting her arms to try and work out the kink in her neck. *Amanda would know what it's all about. Speaking of Amanda ...* Clara pulled out her phone and shot off her promised text.

Clara: Made it across the pond. Heading to the hotel now. Probably won't text you again until we meet for dinner.

~

It was nine thirty a.m. London time, and the morning commute was still underway.

"Just like back home," she mused to her London cab driver.

"Oh? And where is home for you?"

"Southern California."

"I visited there with the missus a couple years back. I'd wager that your traffic is indeed worse than ours." He looked at her in his rearview mirror. "Once we're away from Heathrow and on the motorway, traffic should thin out. We should arrive at your hotel about ten thirty or eleven a.m. Until then, enjoy the ride."

For the first time since finding out her flight was delayed hours before, Clara released some of the pent-up stress from her body. She'd arrived in London and was on her way to the hotel. Sitting in traffic, there really was nothing more she could do but relax. A colossal weight had been lifted off her shoulders.

"Would you mind taking the most scenic route possible?" she asked. The cab ride was on the airline, so why not indulge herself a little?

"Yes, miss." The taxi driver grinned. "Are there any specific sites at the top of your list you'd like to see?"

She shook her head. "Whatever you think a first-time visitor to the city should see would be great."

At first, the car inched along away from the airport from one roundabout to another. But as soon as they entered the London city limits, the landmarks they passed captivated her. They drove past Trafalgar Square, Nelson's Column, the Houses of Parliament, and Westminster Abbey, sending chills of excitement up her body.

"On your left is Big Ben. Its formal name, however, is the Elizabeth Tower. Most Londoners set their watches to Big Ben. I suggest you do the same." The driver pulled out to the right-hand lane to let Clara soak in the view.

She made a mental note to return here at a later point in time with Amanda. *This would be the perfect spot for a photo shoot in my tutu. I could get the London Eye and an iconic red phone booth in the background too.*

Letting a cherry-red double-decker bus pass the car, the driver reentered the traffic, and drove over the River Thames.

"Is the water always so mucky?" It was a muddy dark brown, matching the coloring of the Houses of Parliament. "I always thought it would be a little clearer."

"It really depends on the time of year." The cab driver chuckled. "The short answer is yes, it's usually brown. The Thames hasn't been clean for a century or two. You know, if you stroll down by the embankment, sometimes during low tide, you can even find some Victorian-era rubbish, like tobacco ends." He slowed the car once more. The street was lined with flapping Union Jack flags. "I can't turn in or get too close to it, but up ahead is Buckingham Palace."

"Wow," she breathed out softly. Viewing the gilded gold unicorn and lion on the gates of the formal entrance to the palace sent a jolt of energy up her arms. Butterflies fluttered in the pit of her stomach.

Tourists darted in front of the cabbie before the signal changed colors, like ants swarming a picnic. The area was even more chaotic than Heathrow Airport. "There are so many people around here. I wonder how the royals get in and out?"

"They have a police escort. All the movements and appearances of the royal family are usually carefully choreographed, except for the Prince of Wales." The driver shook his head. "He's always popping up in unexpected places. The media loves him for it."

Clara wracked her brain. All could remember was that the Prince of Wales's name was Prince Edmund. And that was only because Amanda happened to have the world's biggest crush on him. He was her "future husband."

Before she could ask another question about the royal family, the taxi arrived in front of a beautiful flat-fronted red-brick Edwardian home that had been converted into a hotel.

"Thank you so much for all of your help! You've really set the scene for my stay."

The driver walked around the car and opened the door for her. She handed him the entire stipend Pacific Skyways had given to her.

"Thank you, miss. It's been a real pleasure. Enjoy your

stay in the UK. I hope this is the first of many visits for you."

With no luggage to worry about, Clara settled her travel purse on one shoulder, tutu bag under the other, and walked up the set of four steps into the lobby area. The foyer contained rich mahogany-colored walls, checkered-patterned floors, and portraits of the family who must have once lived in the home.

To the right of the lobby, she smelled fresh floral arrangements and eyed two comfortable wingback chairs settled in front of a cozy fire. Crystal chandeliers adorned the ceilings.

"Welcome to the Central London Hotel in Victoria. Can I be of assistance to you?" the doorman inquired, taking Clara's belongings from her hands.

"Oh thanks! I'm here to check in. Where can I find the front desk?"

"Right over there, miss." The attendant motioned for her to follow the hallway to the left into the lobby.

"Thanks." She skipped over to the front desk.

Chapter Three
CLARA

"I'm sorry, miss. The room reservation was made for Maria Tsukyskia, and shows up in our system as canceled as of two days ago. Do you have a different reservation number I can check for you?"

Clara was on the verge of pounding her head against the sleek marble desk, her frustration mounting. A vicious tension headache was building behind her eyes.

"The only info I was given was that the room was supposed to have been transferred into my name. I'm stepping in for Maria in the World Stars of Ballet gala. There should be a block of rooms here for all the performing artists."

Clara frantically swiped through her email. Maybe she was truly living in the twilight zone. Was it possible her room reservation didn't exist?

"Unfortunately, I can't confirm anything due to privacy restrictions. The best I can do is suggest for you to reach out to your group contact and see if they can help straighten the matter out."

"Let me make a call. Excuse me for just a moment." She gathered her belongings and stepped to the side so the next person could check in.

With shaking hands, she typed in the number for Igor Radovsky, the gala's coordinator.

Please pick up, Igor, please pick up!

"You have reached the voice-mail box of..."

She waited for the beep. "Hi, Igor, this is Clara Little. I've made it to London, but there is a small misunderstanding at the hotel that I need your help with. If you can get in touch with me as soon as you receive this, that would be great. Thanks!"

Her shoulders hunched as the clock in the lobby chimed noon. She had three hours to figure something out. *I've pretty much hit rock bottom. I don't think I can sink any lower than this.*

Taking a moment to center herself, she placed a hand on her chest, closed her eyes, and visualized all the stress of the day leaving her body. She counted to ten and released her breath. Feeling somewhat more composed, she returned to the front desk. The same clerk was still available and signaled her over to him.

"Sorry about that. I just left a message with my group contact." She dry swallowed. "Do you have any available rooms for one night in case he doesn't get back to me?" If she paid for the room on her own, she could have the gala group reimburse her.

The clerk tapped on his keyboard and fixed his gaze on the screen. "We have an executive suite." He paused. "Actually, it appears that's the *only* room remaining." He pulled out a calculator and typed the rate onto the keypad in front of her.

Clara's eyes bulged. "And that's for *one* night?"

"Yes."

For a girl who only had a thousand dollars in her savings account, that wouldn't even cover half the total! The limit on her emergency credit card was three grand. If the total included tax, she could just barely manage it, but if anything else went wrong, she'd be SOL. She'd better not take any chances.

I guess what I need is caffeine and a place to sit while I figure out what to do.

As politely as possible, Clara explained to the clerk that she would not need the room after all. Her cheeks burned. "Do you know where I can find the closest café?"

"There's the hotel tearoom, a pub next door, and a Norma's Café down the way."

"Thanks."

∽

Stepping into the hotel's adjoining pub, Clara swept her gaze around the bustling room. Every table was taken by sharply dressed men engrossed in conversation. She unconsciously licked her lips. As a ballerina, she was accustomed to being surrounded by men with nice physiques, but a well-fitted suit on a strong body was her definition of sexy. Her list of things she loved about the UK was growing.

As discreetly as possible, Clara snapped a photo of the three men standing closest to her.

Clara: You have to see it to believe it.

Message sent, she tucked her phone away, and glanced around for a place to sit.

Well, there isn't anything in here, but maybe back there?

She held a hand to her forehead and squinted. A few seats were upturned and placed on top of tables in the back corner, likely reserved for use later in the afternoon. Did this mean there was an additional room back there? There was only one way to find out.

Chapter Four

DAVID

"Everything all right back here, gents?" inquired Stephen, the pub manager and a retired member of the Prince of Wales's security detail, as he poked his head in to check on his former charges.

"As well as can be expected," responded Prince David, the Duke of Leeds. "We could do with another pitcher of water."

"Coming right up." Stephen smirked and brought back the requested pitcher with speed that rivaled the fastest racehorse at Royal Ascot.

"Thanks." David nodded in appreciation, then turned his attention back to his cousin Eddie, who sat at the table with his forehead resting on top of his arms. David furrowed his brow and crossed his arms, leaning back in his chair.

"I'll be in the bar area catching up with the blokes if you need me," Stephen offered, referring to David's and Eddie's security details. He was well-versed in the art of disappearing.

Since Stephen had taken over the Red Lion pub, it had

become a favored spot for members of the royal family to frequent. He always kept the pub's back room unoccupied and at their disposal. David had never felt more grateful to the man.

"Eddie, I understand you've had a terrible letdown with Sadie, but you're still in your early twenties. This wasn't your first relationship, and undoubtedly, it won't be the last," David stated in a weary but composed tone.

How can I get through to him? He rose and began to pace the room.

Eddie glanced up from the table, his eyes red-rimmed and cheeks flushed. He stumbled to his feet, and his chair toppled to the ground.

"You're in league with my parents! They're always pushing me to consider how my behavior will appear to the bloody press! I'm the Prince of Wales. I can do whatever I please, whenever I please."

"Eddie, you told me you had an emergency. I jumped on the first plane from America to London to be here for you." David pinched the bridge of his nose. "Do you have any idea how much trouble it was to have to coordinate a last-minute flight? I've had to cancel or reschedule all my meetings. I was representing the UK on a state visit to America."

He sighed and removed his glasses, rubbing his tired eyes. He'd been up since four a.m. Los Angeles time. He longed for his bed, but he knew it was his duty first to see to his cousin. Uncle Reg was going to tan his hide for giving in to another one of Eddie's tantrums.

"Understanding women can be notoriously difficult. There's a reason I'm still a bachelor." David fought off a yawn, attempting once more to reason with his cousin. "Do you recall how my own last relationship ended?"

Eddie shook his head.

"Elsa dumped me right in front of the media on Ladies' Day at Royal Ascot. She told me that I lacked any personality and called me a human robot. The media had a field day. I've never been able to shake off the moniker 'The Boring Royal.' I thought everything was going well, and we were well-suited to one another, but as it turns out, I had completely misunderstood her. How do you think that made me feel?"

His cousin shrugged and stared at the ground. David walked over to Eddie and placed a hand on his shoulder. "Answer me this: How many serious relationships have you had? This was the first romance I can remember lasting more than four months."

Was it even four months? He'd lost count.

"Does it matter? She broke my heart!" Eddie whined, downing a shot of water. "I gave her Cartier jewelry. I took her to Paris, Milan, Berlin… everywhere she asked me. How could she just pack up and leave me for Jerry, a soddy *underwear* model? Do I not look toned enough in just my boxer briefs?" Eddie fumbled with his belt and was stopped by David.

"Eddie, I'm not even going to touch that question." He cleared his throat and adopted the same authoritative tone his uncle favored. "Here's what's going to happen. Your detail is going to take you home. Once you've had time to sober up, we'll discuss what's comes next in a rational manner." David moved next to Eddie, knelt down, and rubbed a few soothing circles on his back. "You're like a brother to me. I'll always be here for you no matter what, but this is the last straw. It's time for you to grow up."

Eddie's face took on a slightly green hue. "I think I'm going to be sick."

He wobbled to his feet. David abruptly stood and moved out of the way as Eddie rushed past him toward the loos, colliding into several tables near the room's entrance. The sound of shattering glasses and ceramic plates filled the air, making him wince.

Just as David looked up, he watched in slow motion as Eddie crashed into a petite woman attempting to enter the room. She fell, hitting the ground with an audible thud. He froze, his pulse racing. Who was she and where had she come from? Forcing himself not to panic, he sprinted over to the woman, trying his best to avoid the shards of broken glass.

Two members of David's security detail scrambled into the room amidst the chaos. He instructed one of them to check on Eddie, and for the other to assist him. He knelt down beside the woman. Her eyes remained firmly shut.

"I am so sorry, miss. Can you hear me? Where does it hurt?" he asked, waiting for a response. His eyes scanned the woman for any outward sign of an injury. Something about her appeared oddly familiar. Where had he seen her before?

"I'm done. Just done. Everything that can go wrong has gone wrong." A steady stream of tears suddenly made their way down the woman's face. She groaned, and her eyes opened. "Can we fast-forward through the rest of the day?"

David stared into the most stunning shade of hazel eyes he had ever encountered. He couldn't look away. He repeated his question. "Where does it hurt?"

"Everywhere, but I'm used to that." The woman shifted slightly. Slowly and methodically, she shimmied up into a sitting position, resting against the nearest wall for support.

David watched her closely. She blinked a few times, and her hand went to her forehead. He reached over and took her hand in his. A jolt of electricity shot through his body, causing him to immediately release it.

Her eyes went wide, and their gazes locked for several seconds. Her chest rose and fell. The gold flecks in her hazel eyes reminded him of the warm sunshine.

"Sir, shall I ring Dr. Evans?" the remaining security officer asked.

He blinked slowly. "Yes. Straightaway."

He reached for the wad of paper napkins on the ground. "I need you to stay still for a moment. You, er… have a small cut on your forehead," he said, brushing back a few stray hairs and gently patting the cut. "It looks like it might just be a surface scrape."

He was going to have a *very* serious conversation with Eddie after this.

Chapter Five

CLARA

For the first time since she had been knocked over, Clara felt more aware of her surroundings. The man assisting her had the clearest blue eyes she'd ever seen. They reminded her of a tropical beach, where the water was so clear, a person could see the fish swimming, and the sandy bottom.

"I think I can take it from here," she said, holding the rough paper napkin on the scrape. Clara took in the sight of the broken dishes. "Would you mind helping me to a chair, though? I think we'd both be more comfortable if we weren't sitting on the floor."

"Right. Of course," he said.

He wrapped his arms around her, lifting her with ease. If the situation hadn't been so serious, she might've made a joke about recruiting him to be a pas de deux partner. She breathed in the scent of sandalwood and expensive men's cologne.

He deposited her in one of the few chairs standing upright near her, then unbuttoned his suit jacket and draped it over her shoulders. The material was surprisingly lightweight.

She rubbed her fingers over the sleeve. "Linen?"

He nodded. "Yes."

As he ran a hand through his hair, the fabric of his dress shirt shifted, outlining defined muscles in his chest and arms. There was no question that the man was fit.

"I'm so, so sorry for what just happened. When I think about the damage that my irresponsible cousin—"

The room started to sway, and she saw fuzzy spots. Her body felt too warm. She removed the jacket from her shoulders and fanned herself.

The man was by her side in an instant. She heard the sound of water being poured. The stress of the day had finally caught up with her, becoming overwhelming. The room felt like it was closing in.

The flight. The luggage. The hotel. I'm cursed.

"I need… I need some air," she managed to stammer, feeling as if she couldn't breathe.

The man quickly helped her to her feet, guiding her to a chair out on the pub's patio. Clara focused on taking slow, deep breaths, trying to regain control of her racing heart and frantic thoughts. A sense of embarrassment and vulnerability surged through her, making her feel small and exposed.

Away from the chaos of the room, the man served as a comforting presence, offering a reassuring touch on her arm. It wasn't lost on Clara that he understood words weren't necessary.

The cool breeze hit her face. She closed her eyes and focused on taking even, steady breaths.

Inhale. Two. Three. Four. Exhale. Two. Three. Four. Inhale. Two. Three. Four. Exhale. Two. Three. Four.

A few minutes passed and her breathing returned to normal.

She looked up into two pools of deep blue, grateful for his understanding. "Thank you," she said, her voice still shaky but sincere.

He appraised her with a look of concern. "Are you feeling a bit better now?"

Clara nodded, feeling a mix of embarrassment and gratitude. "Yes, I am."

"Would you like me to fetch you a glass of water?"

She nodded. "You don't have to bring it to me, though. I think I can go back inside."

"Only if you're sure. I promise, it's no trouble at all."

"I'm positive."

Stumbling to her feet, Clara allowed the man to take most of her weight as he guided her to the closest chair. Wordlessly, he poured her a cool glass of water.

"I'm so embarrassed. I haven't had a panic attack in years. I'm sorry for the trouble"

"It's nothing to be embarrassed about. It can happen to anyone." He rubbed a few circles on her back. "Only one person needs to apologize, and that's me."

That voice! That's why he looks so familiar. She studied the man clearly for the first time.

At the same time, a light of recognition brightened his eyes. "You saved me at the airport, and I never thanked you properly. You caught me at the moment I'd realized that I'd misplaced my wallet. My security team thought it would be amusing to watch me struggle. I was annoyed and acted like an arse to you."

"It's not a big deal." Clara closed her eyes and rolled her shoulders. "Although if you wanted to pay me back—"

"I'll buy you anything."

She opened her eyes. "Something to eat would be appreciated." She reached for the cup of water and took another glass. "I think part of the panic attack was triggered by hunger. I've been so busy trying to sort out all my problems that I haven't had time to eat anything since we landed."

The gentleman in front of her frowned. "That was hours ago."

"I know," she admitted sheepishly.

"What would you like?"

"A sandwich?"

"I'll do you one better than that." The man whipped out his mobile and sent out a text message. "What about drinks? Water? Tea? Juice?"

"Just water."

He disappeared for a moment.

Clara set the napkin down on the table and drank once more. She let out a deep breath, assessing her body. Her head was achy, her neck stiff, but manageable. Her back felt fine, and her arms and legs seemed all right. As she pointed and flexed her ankle, however, a sharp twinge of pain shot through her foot, and she hissed involuntarily. Glancing down, she spotted blotches of purple and green, the beginnings of a bruise.

"No. No. No." She face-palmed. "How am I going to dance on this?" She started to stand, intensifying her pain.

The man reentered the room. "Please, stay seated until you've been checked over by Dr. Evans."

"I don't have time to see a doctor. I have somewhere to be at three."

"You have time." He reached into a trouser pocket and checked the screen of his phone. "It's twelve thirty-five."

Clara's breathing eased. "Okay... might be true, but I

can't just sit around and wait for a doctor. I have things to do."

Knock! Knock!

"Enter," the man said.

"Sir, we have the food you requested." A clean-shaven man with close-cropped salt-and-pepper hair came in pushing a room service trolley containing several silver platters.

"Thank you, George, please leave that here. Has Evans indicated if he's on his way? This woman—" He cocked his head to the side. "Uh... what's your name?"

"Clara."

"Clara should be seen before Eddie. She's on a tight deadline."

"Yes, sir. Dr. Evans was on the motorway the last we heard from him. I can ring him again if you'd like."

"Please and thank you."

George departed the room.

"And.. your name is?" Clara asked.

"I'm David." He gestured to the platter on the table. "By all means, eat."

"This is for me?" She blinked twice.

"Well, it isn't for me," he said in a dry tone.

She lifted the top of the silver platter. There were tea sandwiches, scones, fresh fruit, and deviled eggs. Peeking under the other platters, Clara discovered a selection of cold meats, crackers, and desserts.

"This all looks so good; I'll start with these," she said, helping herself to two tea sandwiches and some fruit.

"Are you staying here? After you eat, if you want to head up to your room to have a lie down, I can send the doctor up as soon as he arrives."

"I'm not sure yet... that's one of the problems I'm trying to figure out."

"That won't do." With three powerful strides, David crossed the room. He whispered something to George, then came back. "I sent George to speak to one of the front desk agents. He'll straighten out whatever's going on."

Clara thanked him and continued to eat. Eventually, she said, "This is, by far, the strangest day I've ever had. Is your cousin okay?"

"He'll be fine. He just needs a good night's sleep." David removed his glasses and inspected the lenses. "I just hope his father doesn't find out about today's mess until Eddie's had some time to—"

"Sir, pardon the interruption. Here's the gent from the front desk, just as you requested."

"Brilliant. Thank you, G."

The clerk who had assisted Clara earlier hunched, making himself appear smaller. "Ms. Little, you shouldn't be here..." The clerk trailed off and mopped his brow.

"Never mind that. She's here as my guest." David spoke with authority. "Can you give us an update on the status of her room?"

The clerk kept his head down and mumbled something, making him difficult to understand.

David stepped in front of Clara, as if shielding her from the clerk. She was reminded of a fierce lion. "Enunciate, man, and speak up. We can't clearly understand a word you are saying."

"We apologize, Miss Little. It appears that earlier, there was some type of computer glitch." He stuttered and struggled to get the words out at first. "Your reservation was never actually canceled. Since no one ever checked in and the room was left unoccupied yesterday, it was given away.

We're still fully booked, but I've taken the liberty of speaking to one of my colleagues over at our sister property in Kensington. We're able to accommodate you there."

Clara felt deflated as she sunk into the back of the chair.

New plan. Do not pass go. Do not collect two hundred dollars. Go straight to the Royal Opera House.

"That's the best you can do?" David challenged.

"Yes, sir."

David lifted his chin. "Thank you for informing Ms. Little," he said, his tone clipped. "It seems she won't be requiring your services during her stay in London. My family will see to her." He turned to George. "Please have Paul settle the bill for our entertainment, including the collateral damage, with Stephen."

Clara breathed in and out. "Thank you for your generosity, but that isn't necessary." She bit back a wince as she stood. "I appreciate the kindness, but I really wouldn't feel comfortable accepting any more help from a stranger I've just met."

Turning toward the shocked-looking clerk, she continued, "I have no problem staying at your Kensington property. Just give me an address, and I'll figure it out later."

"I promise, there are no strings attached." David's eyes crinkled, as if he were in the midst of a joke. "You were kind to me in LA, and now I'm repaying you."

"You gave me food. As far as I'm concerned, we're even."

"No. We're not even close to being even. Look, if you are worried about being with a stranger, my staff can vouch for me."

She rolled her eyes. "If you pay their salaries, of course your staff is going to speak highly about you."

Clara's heart told her to shut up and accept the offer,

yet her brain said to be cautious. David was obviously some type of important millionaire. He was probably used to getting whatever he wanted, and people saying yes to him, but she had principles.

"That's true..." He rubbed the back of his neck. "Would you trust the word of a doctor? He's known me since I was a child."

"Yes?" She appraised him. David didn't strike her as the type of man who threw money at his problems. From her perspective, he seemed genuinely concerned.

George, the man who delivered the food to her earlier, stepped forward and cleared his throat. "Miss, please trust His Royal Highness. Leeds was one of my commanding officers in the military. I served for just under twenty years, and I left the army to come and work for him because I have an immense respect for him. Trust me when I say that there is no finer gentleman."

David's neck flushed a shade of light pink. He stared at a piece of broken glass on the ground.

"Whoa, wait a second. You're a... a... royal?" she sputtered, taking a few steps back. "It's official. When I stepped off the plane, I didn't land in London—I landed in Wonderland."

I really wish Amanda were here right now. We could switch places. She's the one who keeps up with the happenings of the royals and celebrities. Not me. The only thing that really matters to me is becoming a principal dancer. Other than that, I like my life to be low-key and to fly under the radar. I don't want to get involved in any drama. The royals are magnets for that.

"I'm not looking for any trouble. I'm a person who you probably wouldn't even normally give a second glance to. I just need to get to rehearsal, eat, perform, then sleep."

David's head shot up. "So you want *nothing* to do with me *because* of who I happen to be related to?"

"Basically, yes," Clara answered.

His eyes widened. "I was raised to be a gentleman. If you want nothing to do with me, I can understand and respect that. But"—David took a step closer to her—"will you at least allow me to make sure that everything for the rest of your stay in London goes smoothly and that you're physically, okay? You wouldn't have to see me again. My staff can handle everything."

Something about the clear, bright cerulean-blue eyes behind the glasses made her relax. She instinctively knew she would be in safe hands under his care. The sight of David's pleading expression tugged at her heart.

I'm too exhausted to fight him. I would love to have the rest of my time here be smooth sailing.

"Fine. You've convinced me."

David's lips curved up. "I promise, you won't regret it."

"I'd hope not."

"George, if you could please have the car brought around to the front. We'll head over to the Saint George Hotel in Mayfair."

Clara shifted her weight. The throb in her foot was becoming increasingly difficult to block out. She was accustomed to the aches and pains that came with dancing professionally, but this type of pain wasn't normal. It currently felt like a sledgehammer had been dropped onto her foot. Getting through tonight was going to require a Herculean effort.

David's forehead creased as he assessed her. "Will you let me help you walk out of here?"

"As much as I hate to admit it, I don't think I have much choice," she said, her jaw clenched. She tried to put the full amount of weight onto her foot and almost came crashing to the ground.

David acted swiftly and caught her. For the second time that afternoon, she allowed him to carry her, resting her head against his shoulder. It was a position that felt natural, warm and cozy, like a cat curled up on a fleece blanket in front of a fireplace.

"I'll fetch some ice once you're in the car. It's a short trip."

"Perfect," she whispered. Her lids grew heavy. Her breathing evened out, and she fell into a dreamless sleep.

Chapter Six

DAVID

David's own body was running on fumes. How long had he been awake? He could vaguely recall receiving a voice mail from Eddie and asking the embassy staff to cancel or reschedule his remaining engagements. Had it all happened in the same day?

"Sir?" His lead protection officer angled his body so it faced the back seat.

"Yes, George?"

"If you'll secure your seat belts, Michael can start the car and get going."

He face-palmed. "Right, sorry."

Being careful not to jostle the sleeping Clara, he pulled the seat belt over the blanket he'd tucked over her and secured it. As he watched the woman sleep, he was smitten by the vision in front of him.

She looks like she could sleep for a hundred years. He gently brushed a stray bit of her long dark-brown hair off her face. *I know I promised that I'd stay out of her way while she's here, but I can't let that happen. There's something about her that's so special. I want to unravel everything there is to know about her.*

"Sir?"

His face seared with heat. He moved over and buckled up. "All set."

"You're wondering how to spend more time with her, aren't you?" George asked.

"Is it that obvious?"

"Sir, you're an open book." The car pulled out into traffic. "You've been staring at her nonstop since you first set eyes on her."

"I've never been so attracted to a woman before, and especially to someone whom I've just met."

"Perhaps it's the fact that she declared she didn't want to associate with anyone with a title."

"That's a large part of it, yes."

"If you don't mind me asking, sir, how do you plan to proceed?"

He's still a military man at heart. There isn't any skirting around the issue. With George, it's straight to the point.

"I'm crossing my fingers that Dr. Evans can put in a good word for me." He scratched his forehead. "If he just so happens to hit it off with Clara and invite her around to a family dinner, who knows, I might be close enough to drop by. After all, I have a long-standing open dinner invitation."

George grinned. "Thinking positive is always a good thing, sir."

"I'm glad you think so, because that's only a part of the plan."

"And what's the other half?"

"It involves Michael."

"Uh-huh." The driver, who had been silent but following the conversation, now chuckled. Like George, Michael had also served in the Household Cavalry with David. "And what's my assignment for the next few days going to be?"

He glanced over at Clara's sleeping form. "Clara's a first-time visitor to London. She's going to need transportation around the city, and there's no better way to travel than by private car with a driver who knows the city intimately."

Michael laughed. "You seem to have thought just about everything through."

"It comes with the territory have having gone through Oxford and Sandhurst," David said smugly.

"Actually, I think there's one detail Leeds may have overlooked." George grinned.

"What's that?" David asked.

"What are you going to tell you mother?" George deadpanned.

He groaned. *How could I forget about Mum? Who knows what she'll do if she picks up any inclination about my interest in Clara.*

"Your mother has the nose of a bloodhound, she does. Good luck trying to keep it as a secret." George looked into the rearview mirror from his position in the front passenger seat.

"Sir, George is right about that," Michael said. "If the Princess Royal has it her way, she'll be planning your wedding before the end of the year. Perhaps you can get your uncle on your side for reinforcement."

His mother would do anything to see him settle down and become a married man. The only person who had any measure of control over her was his uncle Reg. Michael was right. He needed his help.

Could I have found a person who wants to know me and not the prince?

Chapter Seven
CLARA

Clara felt her body being shaken as if no time had passed. She didn't want to move. Her dream had been so pleasant, standing atop the dome of Saint Paul's, soaking in the view of London's skyline. Why did it have to end?

"Clara... I need you to wake up," David said. "Dr. Evans is waiting to see you. You're in the Rose Suite at the St. George. It's one of the most historic hotels in the city, and it'll be your room for as long as you're in town."

She yawned and stretched, sitting tall atop the softest bed she'd ever encountered. "This has to be hands down the most beautiful hotel room I've ever been in." The room she currently occupied boasted a soft-gray, pink, rose-red, and white color scheme. Glancing around, Clara noted there was also a television, large dresser, two fully stocked bookshelves, and a small sitting table. Her entire apartment could fit into this one room.

"I'm happy to hear you approve of it. Your room keys are on the nightstand to your left, with some aspirin and water. Nancy is the head maid of both of the hotel's penthouses. Press one on the room phone to speak with her at any time."

"What time is it, please?"

"It's half one," David said.

Clara's adrenaline surged. Now fully awake, she scooted toward the edge of the bed, careful not to jostle her foot. "Where's my tote bag and my costume? I have to get going."

"Woah. Hold on a moment. We went through this earlier. Dr. Evans is here to see you before you go anywhere. I promise, you have time."

Knock. Knock.

A man with thinning red hair and a mustache poked his head inside. "Ms. Little, welcome to the UK. I'm just sorry it's under a set of less-than-ideal circumstances. Allow me to introduce myself. I'm Dr. James Evans."

He spoke with a thick Irish accent, and it took Clara a moment to understand him, but she attributed that to the fatigue. Dr. Evans had perfect posture and an air of command, appearing as if he could remain calm in any situation.

She inclined her head and waved shyly. "It's nice to meet you, Doctor."

"Dr. Evans." David smiled widely and walked over to him. The two men exchanged handshakes.

"Your Highness, I apologize for the delay. I heard that young Edmund had gotten into trouble again. I assumed I would be taking care of him first, not this lovely lady in front of me." Dr. Evans paused and smiled at Clara. "Miss Little, my wife and daughter both hope to see you dance this evening."

"Dance?" David asked. He shot her a questioning glance, his blue eyes widening in amazement.

"Oh yes. Miss Little is a very gifted ballerina from America. My wife has been reading up on your career and watching quite a few internet videos of your dancing since she learned you'd be performing this evening. The Evans women have been looking forward to your performance for the past week. I've heard quite a bit about you at the dinner table." Dr. Evans's eyes twinkled in mirth. "As sad as my daughter was to hear about the Bolshoi's prima being out, my little Jenna was even more excited to hear you would be replacing her."

Clara's pulse beat quickly against her ribs. "Doctor, I have to be at rehearsal at three."

"Then I'd better hurry it along. I know just how important rehearsals are for dancers."

"I'll just, er... take my leave and give you two some privacy," David stammered, starting toward the door. "Clara, I... I'm truly sorry for earlier." He bowed his head, and started to close the door.

It suddenly hit her that this was goodbye. When David walked through that door, she wouldn't see him again. In spite of her better judgement, she called out, "David! Wait!"

He pivoted. "Yes?"

"Um... I... that is to say..." *Why is it so hard to find the right words?* "I hope our paths will cross at least one more time in the next couple days."

"I'd like that."

They held one another's gaze for a long moment, then he slipped out the door.

"I'll be as quick as I can," Dr. Evans reassured her, rummaging inside his medical bag and extracting a penlight. "Let's see what's going on here."

"I'm sorry, Dr. Evans. I didn't mean to zone out."

Clara centered herself on the bed. He clicked the

penlight on and pointed it in her eyes. "Reaction is normal," he noted, and took a closer look at her forehead. "No stitches required, but a nasty little bugger of a bruise will be on your forehead for a few days. Try not to tie your hair back too tightly. What else seems to be troubling you?"

"My foot."

She stretched her leg out in front of her. Clara had always referred to her feet as ugly-duckling feet. The satin pointeshoes that gave the illusion of moving weightlessly across the stage were painful and caused bunions, blisters, bruised toenails, and more often than not, ingrown toenails. She took care to soak her feet in an Epsom salt bath and an ice bath every night, but it was never enough.

Dr. Evans palpated the bones of the foot softly and applied just enough pressure to thoroughly examine it without making it more painful than necessary.

"It's extra tender along your fourth and fifth metatarsals, isn't it?"

Clara nodded.

He sighed. "Without an X-ray, I can only speculate, but I suspect you've fractured both toes."

Her heart sank. Broken toes might not sound serious to the average person, but for a ballerina, it was a disaster.

He removed a set of latex gloves. "My professional medical advice is for you not to dance on it. However, your feet tell me you've danced on worse before."

She nodded again. *He didn't even mention the tendonitis in my Achilles.*

She'd just been promoted to soloist back home. It had been a long road and thousands of hours in the studio to get there. She'd looked forward to finally being able to enjoy the fruits of her labor. The performance season was about to get underway with her company. Yet now, Clara would have to tell her director the dreaded news. She'd be out for at least the next two to three months while the injury healed.

"Since you're *only* dancing a pas de deux, I don't believe you'll exacerbate the injury any further than it already is. As the father of a young ballerina, I understand the precarious situation you're in. Opportunities like tonight don't come often. You're a professional. You're aware of what's at stake. So, I'll leave it up to you to decide. How would you like to proceed?"

"Thank you," she whispered with relief. There was no doubt in her mind. She would dance tonight fully cognizant of the consequences. She released the deep breath she had been holding. "When I take the stage tonight, I'll be performing alongside dancers who are household names. Even if it's only for one night, my name is going to be listed in the same program as them. I may never have another opportunity to show the dance community outside Los Angeles what I'm capable of."

"Please try and stay off your foot as much as possible. You must promise me that you'll rehearse cautiously and not keep on your pointe shoes any longer than absolutely necessary. I'd highly encourage you to ice your foot intermittently until it's time to warm up for the show."

He reached into his medical bag and held up a clear vial. "I'll give you a small dose of a numbing agent."

"I don't want anything strong. It's important for me to be able to feel the floor when I'm dancing."

"Understood." He gestured to the aspirin. "At the very least take two, please."

As Clara reached for the glass of water, Dr. Evans jotted his mobile number down on his business card. "Ring me the second the curtain goes down this evening. I'd like to check you over before you return to the hotel."

She took the card from his hands. "That's awfully kind, but I'd hate to inconvenience you."

"It's no trouble at all. I'll be in the audience this evening with my wife and my daughter. If you need anything during the performance, please send me a message with the ushers. They will know where to find me."

The two talked for a bit longer. Clara was delighted to hear about Dr. Evans's daughter, Jenna, and her schooling at the Westminster Ballet's Upper School. She promised she would meet with Jenna sometime later that week for lunch to give her the inside scoop on life as a professional. Clara always enjoyed being able to spend time with eager ballet students and impart whatever pearls of wisdom she could to them.

A few minutes later, she hobbled around the room, prepping her costume and shoes. Her phone advised that it would take about twenty minutes to make it to the Opera House. If she left in the next few minutes, she'd have just enough time to warm up before meeting her partner for the night, Anton Nicholas. The visit from Dr. Evans took a large load of concern off Clara's plate. Now, she could focus her energy on the reason she'd traveled halfway around the world—the World Stars of Ballet gala.

Chapter Eight

DAVID

David lingered in the hallway as Dr. Evans departed from the Rose Suite. "I'm sorry to bother you, but Eddie's head of security, Myles, just called. He was wondering if you'd be able to swing by Kensington Palace when you were done here."

"I was planning on it." Dr. Evans sighed. "I supposed Edmund will require my famous banana-bag IV drip before he faces his father."

"I've made his excuses to Uncle Reg. Eddie's safe until tomorrow."

"You're kinder than I, Leeds."

Clara opened the door. "David! You're still here!" She pressed her hand to her chest.

"I realized I'd forgotten to mention that my driver Michael is on standby to take you wherever you might like to go."

"If you're sure you can spare him, that would be amazing! I was planning on taking the underground or finding a cab, but a private car would be the ultimate luxury."

"George, would you please see Clara down to the car? I'll wait up here with Dr. Evans until you're back."

George smirked. "Yes, sir." He insisted on taking Clara's bags as he escorted her out of the room.

Once she'd departed, David ran a hand through his hair. "Fill me in, Doc? How is she?"

"You and I both know I can't breach my patient's confidentiality, Leeds. Even for you."

"Will she be healthy enough to dance, though?"

The clues had all been hiding from him in plain sight. How had he managed to overlook that Clara was a world-class ballerina? It was obvious from the way she carried herself.

Even when she's injured, she doesn't just walk, she glides across a room.

Dr. Evans placed a hand on his shoulder. "Miss Little is a professional dancer. She knows her body and knows what it's capable of."

David huffed. "You're not helping."

Her foot is probably the absolute worst place she could be injured. I'm going to make sure Eddie understands that he could've ruined her career. He'll be sending her the world's largest bouquet of flowers to the Opera House tonight.

Dr. Evans's lips twitched. "I'm sorry, lad."

"Well, can you give me a little more information about her dancing career?" David asked.

The doctor's eyes sparkled in amusement. "Mrs. Evans is the clear expert in this area, but I've been privy to a wee bit of information here and there. What would you like to know?"

"Everything."

David was tempted to take notes on his mobile phone, which had been vibrating nonstop for the past two hours.

For the first time in recent memory, he didn't care who was trying to reach him or what the content of the messages was. He was focused on one task—learning everything he could about Clara.

"Miss Little is a soloist at the Los Angeles Ballet Theater."

He cocked his head to the side. "Is that the top rank?"

"No. It's more of a middle rank. One step above the corps de ballet and one below the top rank of principal."

"Where did she grow up?"

"I believe Jenna said something about her receiving her training at the Seattle Ballet Academy."

"Is that a good school?"

"Not that I'm an expert by any means, but yes, I believe it's considered to be one of the higher-rated American dance schools." Dr. Evans blinked slowly. "You know, if you searched her name on the internet, you'd encounter a few videos of her more recent performances."

They chatted for a few more minutes. Doctor Evans shared everything he knew about ballet schools with him.

Soon, one of David's security team members approached. "Sir, your car has returned from Covent Garden."

"Brilliant."

The two men took their leave and rode the suite's private lift to the underground garage. Being able to discreetly arrive and depart from the hotel was one of the many reasons the members of the royal family patronized the St. George.

When they arrived at Kensington Palace, David and Dr. Evans stopped in front of the entrance to the royal apartments 1A and 1B.

"Please stop by or ring me when you've finished with Eddie. I just have some business to catch up with."

"Of course, Leeds, if that's what you wish to call it." The doctor winked.

I'll be checking emails and text messages on my mobile while I watch videos of Clara. Technically speaking, that's business.

David fidgeted. "Do you happen to know if, uh… tickets are still available for the benefit?"

Dr. Evans arched an eyebrow. "Yes, but don't you have access to the Royal Box?"

His body warmed. "Er, yes… I'd… forgotten."

The doctor's body shook with laughter. "I'm sorry, Leeds, I couldn't help myself."

"It's fine." He glanced at his watch. "What time is the show tonight?"

"Seven. But if I remember correctly, I believe your mother is hosting a pre-performance engagement at six."

David stiffened. "My mother is attending?"

"Of course. She's the Westminster Ballet's royal patron. It's been in the papers and all over the company's website—the gala has been on her diary for several months."

He pulled at his collar. There was no chance he'd be able to avoid his mum. *How am I going to explain my sudden new interest in ballet? She's going to see right through me. I'm doomed.*

"Er, thank you, Doctor."

"You're welcome." Dr. Evans started toward Eddie's apartment. "And Leeds? Good luck."

I'll need it. David stood dumbly for a moment, then sauntered up to the front door of his flat. Maybe he could use Eddie as an excuse for once? After all, Eddie always used him as a cover.

David let himself inside. He pulled off his tie and undid the top two buttons on his dress shirt. He slumped into his favorite wingback chair in the first-floor room he used as an office. Pouring himself a shot of brandy for courage, David downed it in one gulp and dialed his mother's private secretary before he talked himself out of it.

Let's get this over with.

"Hi, Mum," he said when his call was connected to her. His voice was a slightly higher octave. He cleared his throat, attempting to make it sound closer to normal.

"David! Well, this is a surprise. Are you all right? Your voice sounds odd," his mother said.

"I just swallowed some water the wrong way." David stood and began pacing the room as they conversed.

"How's your trip to America going?"

"I'm, er… not in America anymore. I flew home this morning."

"You're home? Oh, David, what has Edmund done now? I hope he hasn't gotten himself into trouble again." His mother always seemed to have a sixth sense when it came to her nephew. "The media has only just stopped writing about his last little charade in Paris. I hope we won't be reading about whatever it is this time. Dare I even ask?"

David remained silent. His mother knew them all too well.

"Eddie's girlfriend Sadie ended their relationship rather abruptly. He didn't take the news well," David confessed.

She'd get the gist of it.

His mother let out a sigh. "That boy has had more girlfriends than I can keep up with. Do I need to soften Reggie up before Edmund sees him?"

"That would be the wise thing to do." He removed his glasses. The wheels in his mind spun.

"All right. I'll arrange to have breakfast with him and go riding tomorrow."

"There's something else you should know. There was an incident with Eddie this afternoon. I'm certain no one outside our security details has caught wind of it. But just in case, I was thinking"—he gulped—"that perhaps I might put in a public appearance tonight to help soften the blow if anything *does* slip out." He held his breath, hoping his mother would take the bait.

"I see. And what exactly do you propose?" she asked slowly.

He needed to make a show out of this. "Aren't you attending some big event tonight?"

"Yes?"

"Well, if I joined you, I thought maybe the press would wonder why I was here instead of America. We could have one of our usual sources insinuate that this spur-of-the-moment appearance might have to do with my private life." David waited. The gauntlet had been dropped.

"David, that's kind of you, but I should clarify—tonight's gala is a ballet performance, not an opera. You despise ballet."

"Mum, I was ten years old the first and only time you took me to a ballet. I fell asleep because you and I had just spent fifteen hours traveling the day before. Will you ever let it go? I can behave myself for one evening for Eddie's sake." David had a hard time keeping his glee out of his voice. He couldn't believe it was working.

"Very well. If you insist, come to my flat at five."

"I will." David was struck with a sudden thought. "One more thing: I know that the Evans family usually attends any ballet performances. Would you mind if I invited them to join us in the Royal Box?"

David internally patted himself on the back. He'd have some backup if his mum decided to investigate his sudden interest in ballet.

His mother laughed. "The Evans family were already going to be my guests this evening. I'll see you at five."

David disconnected the call and was relieved to have made it through without giving himself away.

Chapter Nine

CLARA

Clara berated herself for not agreeing to the numbing agent. Meditation and a quick soaking of her feet before rehearsal had helped alleviate some of the pain, but it only went so far. She took several deep breaths, pushing all thoughts of her injury to the far reaches of her mind.

Closing her eyes, she allowed the first few bars of piano music played by the lovely Westminster Ballet's accompanist to fill her body and soul. Her muscle memory took over and guided her through the movements she had performed thousands, maybe even millions, of times.

There was always a sense of peace as she went through pliés, tendus, battements, and frappés. All ballet dancers used the same movements as a basis to prepare their bodies for the day. The barre was the great equalizer. Clara's personal warm-up included a series of abdominal exercises and stretches for her hips, back, and legs. Everything needed to be warmed up to avoid any other injuries.

Her arrival at the Royal Opera House had been relatively smooth, thanks to the easy car ride over. An Opera

House attendant had greeted Clara at the entrance and led her through the maze of hallways to the beautiful studios of the Westminster Ballet.

The Opera House had recently been renovated and was a vast contrast to what she was used to. Large modern dressing rooms and rehearsal rooms littered the building. The Westminster Ballet was a much larger and better-funded company than LABT.

Looking at herself in the mirror, a wide smile graced her face. Dancing on the stage of the Royal Opera House had been her dream since she was a little girl. Every second she spent in the theatre was precious. A dancer never knew just how long their career might last.

At twenty-six years old, Clara was older than the average soloist. She'd spent the past four seasons as a member of the Los Angeles Ballet Theater's corps de ballet. More often than not, a career for was over for a woman by the time she was twenty-seven or twenty-eight years old. Men were luckier; their careers typically lasted longer than those of their female counterparts.

Behind the tutus and the magical satin pointe shoes that allowed the ballerinas to stand on their toes were dancers who pushed themselves to the physical and mental limits of what they could endure. On an average day, Clara was consumed by company classes, rehearsals, and performances from nine in the morning to eleven at night. Her body always experiencing some type of ache or pain that wasn't normal for a person her age.

If anyone were to ask me if it was all worth it, I'd give them a resounding yes. There is nothing more special than being able to dance on a stage, connect with the audience, and become a character in a story.

Closing her eyes, Clara listened to the methodical

sound of her feet brushing along the wooden floors. When she opened them once more after finishing her frappés, she took notice of the tall ginger-haired dancer watching her from the doorway—her partner for the evening, Anton Nichols.

"I'm assuming you're my Aurora," Anton joked as he entered the rehearsal room, coated in a thin sheen of perspiration. Walking over to the barre Clara stood at, he extended his hand to her.

His smile wasn't quite as wide as David's, nor was he quite as tall. Her cheeks warmed. Now was not the time to be thinking of David!

"That's me." Her hands quivered. She wiped her palms against her tights. "I'm so excited to get to work with you! You have no idea how many times I've watched the video of you dancing *The Sleeping Beauty* grand pas with Nela Green. As far as I'm concerned, it's the gold standard." Clara flushed even more. Why had she mentioned that?

He roared with laughter. "Well, I'm happy that you're not afraid to come out of your shell with me. You'll be just fine as my Aurora, especially if you've seen how I like to partner my ballerinas before. Don't be nervous. Igor's assured me you're a quick study. Let's run the pas and see far we can get."

Since they were only two dancers in the room, plus the pianist, Clara was able to relax. There were no outsiders that would be watching and judging her. That would come later tonight.

She covered a yawn with her hand. *Well, at least I'm in character. I feel like I could very well sleep a hundred or more years.*

"Let me put my tutu on and I'll be ready for a go."

Clara hated wearing the heavy "pancake" tutu more

than necessary. She preferred a light rehearsal skirt or a long, flowing, romantic-style tutu. Stepping into the nine heavy layers of tulle, she snapped the garment into place.

She rolled up onto her toes a few times, meeting Anton in the center of the room. A few of the muscles in her legs spasmed, a mixture of excitement and tension. He nodded to the pianist. "From the top."

Anton, a principal dancer with the Westminster Ballet, possessed a rare blend of artistic and technical ability. He had risen sharply to the top of the ballet world. A decade earlier, he had won the prestigious Prix de Lausanne. Dancing with a ballerino of his caliber was a career-defining moment for her.

"Relax," he whispered into her ear.

Her muscles loosened as she melted into his embrace, letting him move her across the floor in sync with the dance's rhythm. In a pas de deux, it was the goal of the male dancer to showcase the female's strength and grace.

He's not just a gifted partner. He's also a gifted coach.

Clara let Anton run the fastest rehearsal she could ever remember. When a ballerina and her partner collaborated for the first time, the differences took time to iron out. Time, unfortunately, was not a luxury the pair had.

The hours spent in the studio on her own time learning and practicing the Westminster Ballet's version of the *Sleeping Beauty* wedding pas de deux was paying off. She could rely on her muscle memory and focus on the dance's details. With Anton, this was working out the timing on the variation's three famous fish dives.

In this intricate move, the male lifted the ballerina, creating the illusion of her diving or swooping gracefully through the air. It took an enormous amount of strength and trust from both dancers.

"Focus on squeezing your hamstring a little more, and fully committing to the dive. The more you lean, the easier time I'll have catching you."

She nodded.

Anton's strength was evident as he expertly performed the skill one-handed. Clara felt a wave of gratitude for his precise technique. She remembered the first time she'd ever attempted the fish dives, her partner had dropped her. He'd blamed her for being too stiff, but in actuality, he had been at fault for misjudging the timing of the skill.

At the end of the forty-five-minute session, they high-fived one another.

"That went about as smoothly as when I run the pas with Nela. You two move similarly." Anton patted his brow with a towel.

"Coming from you, that means everything." She grinned.

"Did you want to have a go at any of the lifts or turns one more time?"

Clara shook her head. "I'm happy to leave it here. I just hope our stage performance mirrors this."

"It will." He winked. "Trust me."

Igor poked his head into the rehearsal room, already dressed for the evening, and nodded. "Bravo. You two dance beautifully. You'll bring smiles to the faces of every audience member."

"I don't think I've ever received so many compliments," she said.

Anton turned to the director. "Igor, you were right to suggest her for Maria's spot. Don't tell her I said this, but Clara here is much calmer, and is so fast to make corrections to the movements."

"She is a true gem."

Clara collected her belongings. "I'm going to head down to my dressing room for a snack, and to get a head start on my makeup."

"Wonderful," Anton said. "I'll meet you on the stage at six. We can warm up together."

Walking out the rehearsal door, she had time to reflect on all that had happened to her.

Today is one for the ages. It's been by far the craziest twenty-four hours of my life. And that's before I even take the stage. David threw me a lifeline by helping me sort out the hotel problems. Oh, I should've asked Igor about that. I'll do it later.

How ironic that she was staying in the Rose Suite in the St. George *and* dancing the role of Aurora. Even if David didn't know it, she'd dedicate her performance to him.

Chapter Ten

DAVID

Flashbulbs exploded, temporarily blinding David.

"Your Highness, look this way, please."

"Prince David!"

He escorted his mother toward the top of the Opera House's steps, passing the red rope line of media personnel.

"…making a rare public appearance with his mother, Princess Charlotte, the Duke of Leeds—one of the world's most eligible bachelors—is dashing in a tuxedo by the rising British designer…"

"…the duke, often dubbed the 'Boring Royal,' made his last public appearance at this year's Trooping the Colour. Regarded as one of the least active members of the royal family…"

He internally cringed. Just because he didn't flaunt his charity work didn't mean he wasn't active. What really mattered was being able to make a difference in a person's life.

David lamented that the headlines tomorrow would focus on the fashion for the evening's event, rather than the performers themselves, like Clara.

"You're attracting quite the female following tonight," his mother teased with a wink.

"Unfortunately."

He waved to the assembled crowd as hundreds of smartphones tracked his every movement. Police in bright yellow vests stood in front of the erected barrier. Finishing the photo call, David and his mother made their way into the theater.

"Your Highnesses, it's a pleasure to host you this evening." Igor inclined his head and bowed at the waist to them.

"Thank you, Igor, I'm very much looking forward to the program you've put together. Such a wonderful cast. We're going to be spoiled." His mother laughed. "This is my son David. David, this is Igor, the mastermind behind the World Stars of Ballet gala."

"Nice to meet you, Igor," he said, stepping off to the side.

"Princess Charlotte. Prince David." The Opera House's director, Lord Cranston, greeted them next.

David acknowledged him. "Lord Cranston."

"If you will follow me, we have a private room set aside for you," the director said.

∽

Forty minutes later, David took his seat next to his mother inside the Royal Box.

"Tonight, you'll be experiencing what's called a mixed bill," she said.

He wrinkled his nose. "Which is?"

"A program that has a variety of performances."

"As opposed to what?" His leg jittered up and down.

"David, tone."

"Sorry, Mother."

"As opposed to seeing a show with a singular theme, like *The Nutcracker*."

"I see."

He stared at the red velvet curtains and watched them sway gently. Was Clara behind there right now? How was she doing? Watching a few videos of her, he wondered how on earth a person could manage to balance on their toes and make it appear so effortless. He'd never again look at any form of dance the same.

I have so much to learn.

"If you find yourself enjoying the dancing, you're welcome to join me at the Westminster Ballet's Upper School graduation performance in a few weeks."

He glanced at his mother. "I'll double check my agenda tomorrow and let your secretary know."

"Excellent, it will be the *perfect* opportunity for you to make the acquaintance of the board of directors. Lady Ferndalehas done such as wonderful job as president."

Where is she going with this? "Uh-huh."

"And of course, Lady Ferndale's daughter, Lady Holly, has recently been appointed the board's secretary. She's a lovely woman about your age. She studied English Literature at the University of Exeter and enjoys—"

So that's the game. Mum is trying to fix me up with Lady Holly.

"Mother, no." He rubbed his temples. "I'm sure she's an amazingly talented and beautiful woman, but I'm *not* interested in going on a date with Lady Holly."

"David, please be reasonable. You're not getting any younger. It's been more than two years since Elsa—"

"We've been through this a hundred times. You

promised you wouldn't meddle in my personal life. I'll open myself to going on a date when the right woman happens to come along."

She didn't need to know that it might be much sooner than she anticipated.

"It's not meddling, per se... it's more that I'm nudging you in the right direction." His mother sighed. "I've been waiting for *years* for a grandchild to spoil."

He blinked slowly. "Trust me, I'm *well* aware."

If there were ever a person who would have made an excellent barrister, it would have been David's mother. She had a way with words and an ability to extract information that David had always wished he possessed.

He studied the evening's program intently and flipped to the page featuring Clara's profile.

"Lovely, isn't she?"

"Who?" he asked.

"Miss Little. I hear she's a star in the making."

"She certainly is," he replied absentmindedly. "She's wasted in Los Angeles." David froze.

"You're acquainted with her?"

"Er... we've crossed paths."

"When?"

He pulled at the collar of his shirt. "Today."

Mother's eyes danced.

He closed his eyes in resignation. He'd been doing so well. *This is why I can't have nice things. I can't hide anything from Mum.*

Like a hawk watching its prey, his mother swooped in with her talons. "Let's both save ourselves the trouble. You'll end up telling your dear old *favorite* mother eventually. Is Miss Little the reason for your newly discovered love of ballet?"

"Partly, yes."

"And the remainder of the reason?" Mother's eyes crinkled. "Is there something you wish to share with me?"

"Yes, but it's not the type of news you're thinking." He took a moment to compose himself. "Eddie's incident I referenced on the phone involved Miss Little."

For a brief moment, his mother's face fell. "Is Miss Little what you might call Edmund's rebound woman?"

"No! Nothing like that." David cringed.

He briefly recounted the events earlier in the day involving Eddie bumping into Clara and injuring her foot.

"I'm proud of you for always looking out for Edmund," his mum said, her face remaining grim. "However, he can't rely on you every time he has a problem. What's going to happen when he enters Sandhurst three months from now?"

David's shoulders hunched. "I don't know."

"He's now twenty years old and a full-on adult. It's time for him to learn from his mistakes and the consequences of his actions." His mother's voice softened. "You've done well mentoring him, but the rest is up to him."

David thought about his own childhood. His cousin reminded him so much of himself. Maybe time in the army was exactly what Eddie needed.

I learned so much about myself and about what it truly means to have people trust you with their lives.

Both mother and son remained silent, contemplating the past and the future for several moments.

"David, circling back to Miss Clara Little—"

He was saved from having to answer mother's question by the sound of the door opening and closing. Dr. and Mrs.

Evans entered the Royal Box with their daughter Jenna. They stood to greet their guests.

"Princess Charlotte, Leeds, thank you so much for inviting us to join you tonight." Dr. Evans smiled.

"James, you know better than to call me Princess Charlotte. Margaret and Jenna, it's a pleasure as always to see you. How is my goddaughter?" David's mother didn't allow Dr. Evans to kiss her hand, and greeted the other Evanses with hugs.

"I'm doing well, ma'am," Jenna answered, trying to hide behind her father as she spoke to the Princess Royal.

"Just like your father," she remarked playfully. "It's Auntie Charlotte. Now tell me about your pointe classes and what variations you're studying."

While his mother engaged in conversation with Jenna about her studies, David made small talk with Dr. Evans.

The Westminster Ballet's orchestra warmed up their instruments, signaling to the audience to take their seats. He discreetly scanned the side of the stage, looking for any sign of Clara. He removed his glasses, cleaned the lenses, then replaced them. Still, nothing. Out of the corner of his eye, he caught Dr. Evans smirking.

"Are you looking for anyone in particular?" he teased.

"No. Just enjoying the view."

His gaze turned to Jenna, the gangly fourteen-year-old, as she slid into the seat next to him.

Was Clara about the same age when she knew she wanted to be a professional ballerina?

His thoughts broke as the conductor entered the orchestra pit to a large round of applause. Glancing around the theater, David was surprised to see it was full, and that the demographic of the audience varied drastically.

When he had come to the Opera House to see *La*

Boheme three months ago, the audience members had been mostly elderly patrons. Tonight, he noticed small children, young adults, and older couples. The array of attire ranged from elegant suits to more comfortable dress slacks.

"So, Jenna, are you excited for the dancing tonight?"

She scooted to the edge of her seat. "Oh yes. Everyone in my class was jealous."

"I have an important job for you tonight." He tried to maintain a serious expression.

She sat taller, appraising him with interest. "What do you need from me?"

He grinned, leaned closer, and whispered into her ear, "It's my first time watching a live ballet in a long time. Do you think you can be my official dance translator? I'm going to have a lot of questions."

"You can count on me for anything."

He pointed to his lips. "It's going to be our secret."

She eagerly bobbed her head up and down.

The house lights fell, the voices of the audience hushed, and their attention turned to the stage.

Clara, I promise I won't fall asleep on you this time. You'll have my full and undivided attention.

The master of ceremonies walked onto the stage. "Thank you for attending this evening's World of Stars Ballet gala performance," he began in a heavy accent. "Tonight, you will be treated to a dazzling display by some of the brightest stars of the ballet world. We hope you'll enjoy this top-notch dancing. There is one change to the previously scheduled program. Clara Little, soloist of Los Angeles Ballet Theater, replaces Maria Tsukyskia from Bolshoi Ballet."

David looked up in eager anticipation as Clara's name was announced. The audience offered polite applause. Why were they so lackluster? Didn't they want to see Clara dance?

The MC left the stage. The audience applauded as the house lights darkened completely. The orchestra took up their instruments and began playing the overture to *Swan Lake* as the curtains opened. David squinted, trying to take in the dancers' faces, searching for Clara.

"This is the White Swan pas de deux," Jenna said.

He felt embarrassed at having to look at his program notes to see what that meant and who the dancers were.

By the third performance, Jenna took pity on him. "Here, you need these more than me." She handed him her opera glasses.

"Thank you." He put them up to his face and continued to watch the performances.

At the intermission, Jenna spoke a mile a minute. "Did you know that every ballerina wears a different brand of toe shoes?"

"I didn't," David admitted.

She wrinkled her nose. "Everyone in my year has to wear the same brand of shoes that the Lower School requires. It's kind of dumb since not everybody's foot can work with the same type of shoe. Like for me, Freeds don't work well. They're too soft and I break them down too fast. At least if I make it into the Upper School, I'll have a choice! I'm really hoping I can try Bloch, Grishko, or Gaynor Minden shoes."

I had no idea fitting a pair of toe shoes could be so technical.

"Ah…"

Jenna launched into a long explanation on the merits of each of the different pointe shoe brands and which brand the top ballerinas wore. Clara wore Freeds.

I wonder if I could learn to make pointe shoes. It can't be that much more difficult than making men's dress shoes, can it?

A bell rang. Audience members returned to their seats, and the houselights dimmed.

Finally, it was Clara's turn. He twisted his rolled program in his hands.

Clara and Anton were announced to roaring applause.

"Anton is the premier dancer here in London. He's taught one of my classes before. He's really nice," Jenna whispered into David's ear. "All the girls dream about dancing with him. Clara Little is so lucky."

So Anton was who the audience was clapping for.

It was silent, and then the first few chords of *The Sleeping Beauty's* wedding pas de deux began. David sat on the edge of his seat. Clara walked regally onto the stage at the same time Anton did. They walked around one another and made a small circle, grasping hands. She stepped up onto the tip of her pointe shoe, her expression that of someone in love.

She looked so different, so poised and otherworldly. He hoped she was acting. Was she in love with this Anton character? Was she really injured? David cringed with each turn, hop, and movement she made, afraid she would collapse at any moment. He clenched the armrests on his chair.

David released his breath as Jenna looked over, took his hand, squeezed it, and smiled. "You need to relax. Dance is an art to enjoy. Don't be so stiff and worried over every movement."

"You are wise beyond your years," he murmured back. Clara wasn't just a performer—she was a storyteller. She moved in sync with the orchestra and used her body to tell Princess Aurora's story.

David glanced over at his mother. He caught the deep respect in her eyes as she watched Clara perform. He was not able to judge the nuances she put into her dancing from watching, but if Clara impressed his mother, a ballet expert, she must be among the elite level of world-class dancers.

Mother is as captivated as I am.

Clara had called herself a workaholic, like David. How long did she spend in the studio every day? He continued to ponder these thoughts while engrossed in the story of Princess Aurora.

Chapter Eleven
CLARA

Clara's pulse beat wildly against her ribs as she stepped out onto the stage, her pointe shoes making a thunking noise against the stage's wooden floor. Her eyes traveled from the conductor holding his baton above his head to the first two rows of audience members. The theatre was dark. She could just barely make out the eerie glow of their face as they applauded politely.

They took their opening marks, and Anton nodded subtly to her. "Breathe," he whispered through his teeth.

The conductor brought his baton down, signaling for the orchestra to play the opening measure of music. Inhaling sharply, she plastered a coy smile on her face and pushed up onto the tips of her toes. This was her time to enjoy the experience. From the wings, other dancers observed her and silently cheered her on. She fed off their energy.

I belong here. I have nothing to prove and everything to gain.

She poured every ounce of contentment and all of her

raw, wild emotions into her performance. Clara was Aurora—a princess who had been kept away from her parents for sixteen years, faced an evil sorceress, stuck a finger on the spindle of a spinning wheel, and was awoken by her prince. All the trouble was behind her. This was Aurora's wedding day, a celebration of good conquering evil.

Aurora and I have a lot in common. We've both experienced the same range of roller-coaster emotions during a long, crazy day.

Clara was halfway through the first section of pas de deux. Mentally, she prepared herself for the upcoming fish dives. If done correctly, they always made the audience gasp and applaud just before the end of the first set of partnering.

Do it just like we practiced.

Clara held herself off-balance, but trusted her much more experienced partner to guide her.

She dived down and allowed Anton to lead her body onto his quad. The first two sets went just fine. Heading into the third fish dive, she knew she was slightly off, and both she and Anton felt her foot start to give way.

Clara didn't have time to be horrified, and just pushed through the unknown. She didn't want to break the performance's spell. She leaned harder than she should've into Anton's leg. He adjusted to her.

"You all right?" he mouthed to Clara. They made their almost final circle, his back turned to the audience.

"Solid," she replied.

On the last set of pirouette turns, she knew she was going to have to improvise. Spur of the moment, Anton read her body language and muscled the turn, gripping the corset above her tutu tightly to completely support her.

The last note hit, she leaped up, and he caught her.

Clara was proud of how much she had managed to fight through the performance. She was close to running on empty. However, she still needed to get through the solo section and the finale. They took their bows, then exited the stage.

Remember to pace yourself, Clara. Slow and steady finishes the race. It's not a sprint. Focus on Aurora. Focus on the audience.

The applause died down as Anton returned to the stage for his solo. The music changed from soft to a more powerful sound and hurried pace.

Anton jumped and turned in the air, showing his polished technique and phenomenal footwork. Clara watched from the wings, trying to savor the moment. She wiped her forehead off with a coarse tissue, limping her way off the stage to where she hoped the audience couldn't see her.

She was tempted to sit on the floor, but knew that mentally, once she went down, she wouldn't get up. She lifted her foot and stretched against one of the portable ballet barres. There was a dull throb that continued to challenge her mental mind block. Knowing her entrance was coming up, she walked over to the closest wing and pounded her legs to try to keep her muscles moving and warm.

The audience yelled, "Bravo!" in approval of their popular premier male dancer. She looked on, walking out as he panted shallowly, using his arms to express to the audience, *If you think my performance was well done, wait until you see my Aurora's!*

Clara took her spot in the center of the stage. The Aurora variation was well known for its steps and choreography. It was one of the most popular variations a younger dancer could learn. Digging deep, Clara refocused once again, using her childhood dream of performing on the Westminster Ballet's stage as her inspiration.

Just breathe and listen to the plucking of the violins and lightness of the music.

In just under a minute, it was all over. She tried to stand tall, taking an extended time to bow and catch her breath. Anton reentered the stage. They began the final ending sequence of the variation. Clara and Anton expertly "talked" onstage and somehow managed to change the direction and which leg she used. Their final turns were by sheer willpower.

They took their final set of extended bows together. Her gaze went to the Royal Box. She wondered if David or any of his relatives were up in the balcony. Yet she didn't have time to ponder her thoughts. Her immediate focus was to take care of her ailing body.

The curtains closed with a whoosh. Her face fell, and she leaned heavily against Anton. The fabric of his top was rough and soaked through. His body was a human furnace.

"I don't think I can make it off the stage on my own," she admitted, and she grudgingly allowed herself to be carried off the stage by him. "I didn't think I would make it all the way through tonight."

The ending was rough. It certainly wasn't my best, but it's going to rank up there as the most emotional performance I've ever given.

"You should be proud. I've never had such a stubbornly determined partner." His forehead creased. "Ankle? Or foot?"

"Both," Clara answered point blank. "Toes and an overstressed ankle. Thankfully, it's not my Achilles."

His jaw tightened. "That's an injury I'd never wish on

anyone. It took me two seasons to make it back to the stage."

Both dancers looked down and could see that her foot was swelling through her tights.

"I'm going to take you up to the physio room. We have a brilliant medical staff that can help make you more comfortable."

"What about the finale? I think I can manage one more go." Clara attempted to wiggle out of Anton's arms.

"No. You're finished for the evening."

"I've already gone this far; you might as well let me take our final bow."

"If you insist, I'll carry you out in a shoulder sit. I refuse to let you walk out on that foot. Think you can manage that?" Anton set her down on a chair.

Clara nodded. "I feel guilty making you do all the work."

"Don't. It's the male dancer's job to take care of his ballerina," he joked. "And besides, one advantage of my being out with a leg injury is that I'm the physically strongest partner on the company's roster." He flexed his biceps.

They shared a laugh.

Chapter Twelve

DAVID

David jumped to his feet and inserted his fingers into his mouth, letting out a shrill whistle. He clapped until his hands were numb.

"Do you have any idea as to how long Miss Little plans to stay in town?" David's mother asking, folding her hands on her lap.

"No, I don't."

"Hmm ... well I suppose it doesn't matter. I'll have Abigail extend her an invitation to afternoon tea in the morning."

"Mother," David warned.

"*I'm* the patron of the Westminster Ballet. It's my *duty* to take an active interest in visiting guest artists." She waved him off. "You're invited too, of course."

David looked away from her. *Dun, dun, dun.* The sounds of trouble echoed inside his head.

Jenna gleefully jumped to her feet as the dancers prepared to come out on stage one last time, startling David and his mother. There was an endless sea of leaps, pirouettes, and other brilliant skills showcased. The audience would be talking about the performance for a long while.

Jenna and David, however, only had eyes for one dancer—Clara.

"She's such a lovely dancer. Her port de bras reminds me so much of some of the videos of Dame Margot Fonteyn," Jenna gushed.

Anton carried Clara across the stage.

The two friends applauded with bravado. It was taking every ounce of David's self-control to keep from running backstage to check in on how Clara was doing.

"Mother, if you don't mind, I'd like to join you and Lord Cranston when the dancers are presented to you."

"I hosted them for a luncheon yesterday. In a few minutes, I'll be heading down to the Grand Ballroom to meet some of the ballet's more generous patrons for cordials. I hope you'll join me."

Mother's tone wasn't asking him. It was commanding him.

"Yes, Mum."

"Excellent." She gathered her handbag and program and moved to speak with Dr. and Mrs. Evans.

His ballerina would have to wait.

When had he started thinking of her as *his* ballerina? Why was he so affected by her? Yes, she was physically beautiful, but there was something else that was drawing him to her. Something he couldn't quite put his finger on.

He ran a hand over his jaw and settled his gaze on Jenna, thumbing through her program.

"Jenna," he muttered, causing her head to pop up.

"Huh?"

"Er… I have another mission for you."

"As long as it doesn't get me in trouble."

He chuckled. "Would I do that to you?"

She hesitated. "You, no. Edmund…yes."

"It's nothing bad. I promise."

She nodded and gave David her full attention.

"Between you and me, I like Clara Little, *very* much." He rubbed his hands together. "Do you think you can find a way to follow your father backstage and check up on her for me? I'd also like you to take note of anything else she tells you, like her favorite foods."

"What's in it for me?"

Eddie had taught her well.

"You get the opportunity to meet Clara." He offered his hand to Jenna. "Do we have a deal?"

David could sense her considering his offer as she rocked back and forth on her heels. "Add in three rounds of playing Mario Kart with me and I'll do it," Jenna countered.

"You drive a hard bargain, but I think those are acceptable terms." They sealed the deal with a handshake and departed to join the others for drinks and dessert.

Chapter Thirteen
CLARA

Although all her reserves had been drained, Clara still felt content and as if she were floating on air.

"Anton, I don't think I'm going to be able to thank you enough for tonight. I've felt so at home here. The last couple of hours has been a real-life fairy tale come true for me."

"I'm chuffed to hear it. I massively enjoyed our time together too. I hope this is the first of many future gigs together. You're going to be one of the first people I ring the next time I need a partner." Anton poked her in the shoulder

"Are you serious? You want me?" Clara splayed a hand on her chest.

"Yes, I want you." He laughed. "If this is how we performed with only one rehearsal under our belt, just imagine all the possibilities with some proper preparation time.

She was at a loss for words. Anton was impressed by her. Little old Clara from Seattle. Her chest swelled. Maybe she was destined to make it all the way to the top and become a principal dancer

A pinching sensation in her foot brought her back down to Earth. Her shoulders hunched as she noticed the ribbons of her shoe digging into her skin.

"Do you think I can ask you for a favor?" she inquired.

"Of course, name it," Anton replied, sounding concerned.

"Do you think you can help me slip my pointe shoe off my franken-foot?" She bit her lip. "It's getting uncomfortably tight, and it's probably going to take two people to yank it free."

Anton knelt down and examined her foot. "It might be better if we can have one of the physios cut it off. Pulling might do more damage." For the second time that evening, he picked her up and carried her into the treatment area.

Doubts and fears swirled in Clara's mind. Dr. Evans had assured her she wouldn't make the foot much worse than it already was, but what if he was wrong? What if she'd made a giant mistake pushing through the pain for nothing? Or worse, what if this turned out to be a career-ending injury?

The weight of uncertainty bore down on her. Clara took a deep breath, trying to steady her racing thoughts. She knew she needed to trust the medical professionals and their expertise. It was their job to guide her through this, to make the right decisions for her well-being and her future as a dancer.

She closed her eyes, attempting to expel all the fear and anxiety. She reminded herself of her passion for dancing, the journey she had taken to get here, and the resilience that had brought her this far. Whatever the outcome, she would face it head-on and find a way to keep pursuing her dreams.

Once upstairs, the excellent physio staff asked Clara to stretch out on a treatment table as they cut and removed the shoe from her foot. Free from its prison, the limb was immediately less painful. It reminded her of changing into a pair of soft stretchy yoga pants after eating a large meal.

"Clara, go ahead and submerge your foot in the rubbish bin while I ring Dr. Evans," the kindly physio said.

She inhaled sharply. Dipping her foot into the freezing cold water, she was filled with sensations of pins and needles. As she gently flexed and moved her foot, she could feel some of the discomfort alleviating. Goose bumps formed on her arms and legs. She rubbed her hands over her forearms.

Dr. Evans entered the room. "Anton, would you kindly grab a blanket for Miss Little?"

He face-palmed. "I should've thought of it."

"I'm fine," Clara said through chattering teeth.

"You're brave for saying so, dear. But the ice is awful. If you can stand it, let's aim to have you ice the limb for five minutes total."

"How did you get here so quickly, or know where to find me?"

"I'm all-knowing?"

"Wishful thinking, Doctor," Anton snorted. "I had one of the stagehands send word to him through an usher." He draped a fluffy fleece blanket over her shoulders. "Is that better?"

"Much." She pulled the ends of the blanket tightly around her, like a superhero's cape.

"Is there anything else I can do to make you more comfortable?" Anton asked.

"No, you've done so much already. I really appreciate it."

"I'm just going to head down to my dressing room and change, then. I'll come and see you before I depart for the evening."

She thanked him.

"Anton's always the gentleman," Dr. Evans acknowledged. He located a dry towel and set it on the treatment table. "I think it's been long enough. Let's have a look at how you're doing."

A few droplets of water splashed onto the ground as she lifted her foot out of the bin. Dr. Evans patted it dry and lightly prodded her toes. Clara attempted look anywhere but her foot.

She caught sight of a young red-headed girl observing them, lingering in the doorway. She glanced from the doctor and back to the girl. They had the same coloring and noses.

"Is that your daughter?"

"If it's a redhead with freckles, and hair to her elbows, yes, that's my Jenna."

"She's beautiful."

"That's all thanks to her mother. I'm afraid I can't take any credit for it." He tested the mobility of her ankle.

"I'm so sorry to pull you away from the show and your family, Dr. Evans," Clara apologized.

"Think nothing of it, my dear. Remember, both of the Evans women are ballet lovers. I just buy the tickets and provide the transportation. I'll be a hero after I treat you tonight. Jenna insisted on following me back here. She's quickly become a fan." Dr. Evans hesitated. "Would you be willing to meet her?"

"Of course," Clara responded enthusiastically.

He spun his chair around. "Poppet, come over here.

There is someone who would like to meet you." Dr. Evans signaled his daughter to join them.

The youngest Evans entered the room carrying a bouquet of pink roses nearly as large as her. The plastic crinkled as she held them up. "These are for you," she said in a low tone.

"Hi, Jenna. It's nice to put a face to the name. Your dad has told me a lot about you. Thank you so much for these, they are gorgeous." Clara took hold of the arrangement. Her eyes fluttered as she sniffed them, and a sweet floral aroma tickled her nose.

"Actually, they're not from me, they're from my friend David."

Clara sat taller. "David was here?"

Jenna nodded. "Auntie Charlotte is my godmother. She's our host tonight."

Clara's eyebrows knitted together.

"Charlotte would be Princess Charlotte, David's mother," Dr. Evans clarified.

"Ah."

Clara's attention returned to Jenna. "Did he... seem to enjoy the show?" Butterflies fluttered in her stomach.

"Yes, but he asked a lot of questions." She covered her mouth with her hand and giggled. "He thought there might be some singing. I had to explain that the gala wouldn't be like the opera."

"As brilliant as Leeds is, sometimes he can be rather clueless." Dr. Evans shook his head.

"Enough about David. What did you think about the dancing this evening?" Clara asked. "What were some of your favorite pieces?"

"I think my favorite was a tie between *Dances at a Gathering* and the *Sleeping Beauty* pas. I really enjoyed the fast footwork Balanchine dancers are known for, but I also loved how graceful and elegant you were when you played Aurora. I hope I can dance like you in the future."

Clara rubbed the back of her neck. "Thank you," she said quietly.

Jenna slowly warmed up to her. The two spent a few minutes discussing the different types of ballet styles and training. Meanwhile, Dr. Evans looked grimly at her foot and returned to examining it.

"Papa, you will be able to help her, right?" Jenna was staring at her father and Clara with a questioning look. "Papa can fix anything. He's the best of physicians."

"Jenna, we think I might have broken my fourth and fifth toes. It's painful, I won't sugarcoat it. Maybe you can distract me while your dad finishes a quick evaluation. Ask me anything."

"What are your favorite foods?" she questioned.

Clara was hungry, and the question about food only made her think about it more. Maybe Amanda would be willing to go over to the St. George instead of them going out for dinner. She needed to text her friend as soon as the doctor was done.

She refocused her attention on Jenna. What foods did she want to try other than fish and chips? Crumpets? Scones? She didn't really know much about British foods.

"Back home, I love having dried mangos, pineapples, nuts, and anything chocolate to snack on between rehearsals. But if we're going for actual food, I'm gonna have to say Hawaiian pizza."

"What's on Hawaiian pizza?" Jenna tilted her head sideways.

"Pineapples, ham, cheese, and tomato sauce. It's the

perfect blend of sweet and salty flavors, which I really enjoy."

"I don't think I've ever heard about someone having pineapple on pizza. I wonder if my friend Jeremy would be willing to taste test it with me."

"Your friend Jeremy will eat anything. He's a human rubbish disposal," Dr. Evans interjected.

"What about local food? Have you tried fish and chips or any curry yet? London has so many yummy dishes to choose from!"

"Not yet, but it's good to know that no matter what I order, it will be good," Clara replied with a smile.

"Jenna, I have to discuss a few things privately with my patient. You know the routine. Why don't you go find your mum and let her know I'll be down in a few minutes," Dr. Evans suggested.

Jenna pouted but agreed. "Thank you for chatting with me." She hugged her father and dashed out of the room.

The bustle of activity from the stage was audible as the door swung open. Clara could hear the theatre techs pulling down scenery and tidying up in preparation for the opera performance the following evening.

Looking at her foot for the first time now that they were alone, she recoiled. It was twice its normal size. Splotches of green, purple, blue, and a few almost-black patches made the foot look like someone had attempted to tie-dye it.

The colors unnerved her, but past experiences had taught her that the bruising was good. It meant the blood flow was getting to the foot, hopefully facilitating a speedier recovery time.

"How serious is it?" Clara asked in a hushed voice, clutching the table's edges with her fingers. "I heard a popping sound when I tried to walk after the variation. My foot felt much more unstable too."

"It is amazing how the human body rallies just when we need it to the most," Dr. Evans remarked. "The fracture feels the same, but there might be some ligament damage too. I'll need to do some scans in the morning. It's a significant injury, but fortunately not one that will derail your career."

A massive wave of relief washed over her. Those were the exact words she needed to hear.

"Stay off of it as best you can. I'll put an air cast on it for now."

Clara sighed and resigned herself to her fate.

All's well, that ends well.

∼

Opening the door to her penthouse, Clara was delighted to see the king-size bed calling her name. She'd refused the services of the butler, but was grateful the staff insisted on carrying her costume and dance bag up to her room upon seeing her return with crutches.

She had forgotten to charge her phone earlier in the day, and the screen was dead. Hobbling to her purse, Clara blindly rummaged around the black void, fishing for her charger and converter plug.

"Success!" she exclaimed to an empty room.

Sinking down on the bed, Clara stifled a yawn. Her phone and plug adapter were now connected to the wall. A slew of text messages loaded as soon as the screen glowed to life. Most could wait for a reply until the morning, but the one from Amanda caught her interest.

I'm terrible. There was so much going on that I completely forgot to text her!

Amanda: Hey, C, I have bad news… I'm not going to make it to London as planned. The entire outbound crew of the Zurich flight is sick. I'm stuck working the turnaround. The airline expects us back at the airport in twelve hours. I'm so sorry. I feel like a jerk, but I promise I will make it up to you. Maybe with a Disneyland trip? I won't say 'break a leg,' but I know you will be amazing. Love you to bits, bestie.

She shot off a short reply just to prove to her friend she was indeed still alive.

Clara: Thanks, A. Exhausted and have so much to fill you in on. The show went as well as can be expected. I'll text you tomorrow. Time for food.

If only Amanda knew how close her words were to the truth. My leg might not be broken, but my foot is.

Clara ordered room service and enjoyed a quick dinner refuel, listening to the sounds of the television in the background before falling into a deep slumber.

Chapter Fourteen
CLARA

K*nock, knock.*
The pounding on the door jolted her awake. Clara rolled to her side, sat up, and rubbed her eyes.

Knock, knock.

A twinge and shooting pain in her foot pulled her back into reality as she tried to stretch her body from its awkward sleeping position.

"I'm coming!" she exclaimed, fumbling haphazardly to the door. Clara cursed her lack of foresight to keep the dreaded crutches closer to the bed.

Yanking it open, she found a uniformed attendant with a small table containing several covered trays. "Room service, ma'am. Where would you like your breakfast?"

Breakfast? I didn't order anything last night? Did I?

"Uh… I guess if you would please wheel the table into the living room?"

"Certainly." He found an empty spot. "His Royal Highness also wished for you to have this card." He passed her an ivory envelope with her name elegantly written in cursive. "Is there anything else I can take care of for you this morning?"

"Um... no thank you, that's all."

"Very well." He let himself out.

Hopping over to the sofa, she turned the letter over in her hand and broke the seal.

Dear Clara,

I hope you're doing well on your first morning in London. I knew that you might be arriving back to the hotel late last night, so I took the liberty of arranging a breakfast spread for you. I hope that it meets with your approval. Please don't hesitate to make the hotel staff aware if there is anything else you require.

Best,

David Leeds

"That has to be one of the most thoughtful gestures ever. Food is one of the ways to my heart," she said to herself.

Curiosity took hold. Uncovering each of the trays, Clara found a spread of eggs, bacon, toast, scones, strawberries, yogurt, granola, mango, pineapple, tea, orange juice, and coffee.

"I have enough food to feed an army."

Her stomach grumbled. Picking up a plate, she tucked into the selection. The coffee tasted as good as it smelled. This was the perfect way to awaken to her first full day in London. How had David known to include some of her favorite foods?

It was ten a.m. when the same room service attendant from earlier appeared to remove the table.

"What's all this?" She blinked several times. The attendant carried a large teddy bear in a frilly pink tutu and an arrangement of blue, yellow, and purple wildflowers. "Are these from the same person who sent me breakfast?"

"Indeed, they are, ma'am," the attendant confirmed.

Taking the bear from his outstretched arms, she hugged the plush toy to her body. Its soft fur felt like velvet against her skin. She sighed in contentment.

"Would you like me to find a vase for your flowers, miss?"

"Oh, yes please." She glanced at the pile of bouquets on the table by the doorway. "Actually, I have a small collection of flowers that could probably use water and vases too."

"I'll collect them on my way out and bring them back to you this afternoon."

"Thank you."

He left the room and the door clicked closed behind him.

"Now just where am I going to put you?" she mused, speaking to the teddy bear. "The bed? The sofa? Hmm…" Ultimately settling on the sofa, Clara took note of a second card attached to the bear's tutu.

Opening the identical ivory white card, she read:

Dear Clara,

By now, I hope you've enjoyed your breakfast and a little lie-in. It slipped my mind yesterday, but when I offered the services of my driver to you, I realized that you might not have a means of contacting him. I've taken the liberty of jotting down a few mobile numbers you might find of use.

A separate piece of paper had the numbers for Michael the driver, Dr. Evans, the hotel, and David himself.

I'm trying my best to honor my promise to you and respect your wishes for me to keep my distance. However, if you find yourself changing your mind, please ring me anytime.

Best,

David

She stared at the elegant swirl and curve of the letters.

They say that a person's handwriting can give you a clue into what type of person they are. I guess I shouldn't be shocked that David's neat, organized, and seems to think of everything. Maybe I was too quick to judge him. That man has gone to so much effort for me.

She located her phone, and just as she was about to call Dr. Evans, she realized that she was still in the same set of clothing she'd worn the day before.

Change of plans.

She dialed the phone in her room and listened as it rang.

"Good morning, Miss Little, this is Nancy speaking. How may I assist you?"

I guess I shouldn't be shocked this line goes directly to the penthouse maid.

"Hi, Nancy, I just wanted to call and see if any luggage had been sent over for me by Pacific Skyways?"

"Just a moment." Classical music filled Clara's ear. "No, Miss Little, there isn't anything yet."

"Bummer."

"Would you like us to follow up with the airline for you?"

"You can do that?" Her eyes widened.

"Yes, as one of our VIP guests, we can do anything you ask."

"Oh wow! Thank you so much." She rattled off the claim number the airline had given her and mentioned there was a chance it might've been delivered to her original hotel.

"Shall I also have the concierge pick out some clothing and amenities for you?"

She was tempted. But then she wondered what might

happen if the concierge bought something outside her price range. She supposed she could charge it to the room and settle the tab later on. Clara considered her next move.

The only normal clothing she had was the outfit she'd worn on the plane the day before. It *would* be nice to have something clean and not have to hobble around London looking for a shop.

"Yes, please."

"Wonderful. If you could please provide me your sizes and style requests, everything will be ready for you within the hour."

"I'm afraid I only know my US sizing, but I usually take a small in tops, a four in jeans, and a seven in shoes. I'm also a fan of blues and purples, but anything will do. I'm a low-maintenance gal."

"Noted, Miss Little. We'll do our best to accommodate your personal preferences. Expect a delivery shortly. Is there anything else I can do for you?"

"No, but thanks for asking." She disconnected the call.

A girl could get used to a life like this.

She reclined on the couch, engaging in a conversation with her teddy bear.

"Since we have some free time…" On impulse, she dialed David's mobile.

He answered after two rings. "Cheers, Clara. How are you this morning?"

She sat up straight, a bit flustered. "David, uh… hi. I, er… I'm doing as well as can be expected. I didn't think you'd pick up. I was planning on leaving you a message. How did you know it was me?"

"A lucky guess. You can thank my watching the telly show *Sherlock* for my powers of deductive reasoning." His low baritone voice let out a throaty laugh. "There are very few people who have this number, and even fewer with an American mobile number."

"You're a *Sherlock* fan?"

"Yes, does that surprise you?"

"Yeah, it does. I had you picked out as a—actually, I've never even really thought about what your taste in TV shows might be," Clara said, playing with the ends of her hair.

"Likewise."

"Just for the record, I don't normally have time for TV, but when I do, it's usually a classic American sitcom from the 1950s like *I Dream of Jeanie* or *I Love Lucy*. My best friend got me hooked."

"Fascinating." She heard the sound of him pouring liquid into a cup. "Now it's my turn to ask. Are you a tea drinker? Or a coffee drinker?"

She bent her knees and used the sofa's armrest as a pillow, relaxing against it. "Coffee all the way, but when I've had too much of it, I'll have green tea."

"That's another similarity we share. I prefer coffee too. I'm not a morning person by nature. I've been told I'm the world's biggest grump when I'm shuffling my way to my espresso machine for my first cup of the morning."

"Do you not care for tea at all?" she said in mock horror.

"I drink tea on occasion. It's programed into my DNA to enjoy a hot cuppa."

They shared another laugh.

"The reason I wanted to call you was to say thank you for breakfast and for the flowers and teddy bear. They were amazing surprises."

"You deserved it. Yesterday was"—he hesitated—"a long messy day for everyone, but especially you. No pun intended, but I just thought you deserved to be treated like royalty for the rest of your UK stay."

"Well, I deeply appreciated it." Clara grinned. "A little red-headed birdy mentioned to me that you attended the gala."

"I did. It was the first time I've seen any live ballet dancing since I was about ten years old."

"And? What did you think?"

"Not that I have much knowledge to go on, but I enjoyed it." She heard David smack his lips and take a sip of his beverage. "If I'm being honest though, there was one dancer in particular who caught my eye above everyone else. Can you guess who it was?"

She sat taller, her heart beating faster. "Me?"

"Yes, you," he murmured.

Her skin tingled. "I, er... that is to say..."

"I know this is a bit presumptive of me, but just keep in mind that if you'd like to have lunch or dinner anytime this week, my agenda is wide open. All you have to do is ring me. I enjoy chatting with you."

"I... I'd like that."

"You would?"

"Yes." A smile tugged at her lips. "I realized that I might've been a little too quick to jump to conclusions about you being a royal." Her cheeks warmed. "It's not lost on me that you're trying hard to impress me. So I thought I'd give you the benefit of the doubt to prove to me you're just another guy."

"Well, brilliant. I—" She heard the sound of him knocking something over. "Ah, bollocks."

"Is everything okay?"

"Yea, I just spilled my coffee all over my trousers."

Knock. Knock.

"There's someone at the door. I'd better get going. I'll figure something out with you after I meet with Dr. Evans."

"You're in good hands with him. And remember, if there's anything you need, don't hesitate to ask."

She thanked him and ended the call. Hobbling over to the door, she found it was Nancy, returned with some much-needed clothing.

∽

Clara stared at the hard purple-and-white fiberglass cast on her foot as Michael drove her back to the hotel from Dr. Evans's office in Wimbledon Common. Dry swallowing, she dialed the phone number for her boss, the artistic director of the Los Angeles Ballet Theatre.

"Hi, Artum!" she said with false cheer. "This is Clara. Thanks for taking my call so quickly."

"Clara! I've seen some early reviews from your gig. They've glowing. You're making everyone here at LABT proud. What's on your mind?"

She breathed deeply. "It looks like I'm going to be out for a couple of weeks. I've injured my foot."

"I see." The artistic director's voice dropped into a flat tone. "How long is a couple of weeks?"

"Seven weeks total. If the fracture heals on schedule, I'll be back by the *Nutcracker* run."

Medically speaking, Clara knew her injury could have been a lot worse. She had a hairline fracture and a torn ligament in the front of her foot. No surgery would be required. It was the best possible outcome. Injuries like this happened all the time. Four weeks in a cast and three weeks in a walking boot would afford all the nagging injuries in her body enough time to recuperate. Except, that wasn't how her AD saw it.

"So what you're telling me is that you'll be missing the entire summer and fall season?"

She fidgeted. "Yes."

"I was counting on you to cover *several* key roles like Giselle and Coppelia, but now you've gone out and ruined everything." Artum muttered something under his breath. "If I hadn't already announced your promotion to the public, I'd take it back right now." He slammed his fist on his desk.

Her jaw clenched. It wasn't like she'd purposefully tried to hurt injure her foot; it was accidentally stepped on. It was all bad luck and ill timing.

"Since you're not going to be able to work, I guess that means I'll have to push the start date of your contract back to January. If you can't dance by then, I don't have a use for you." He abruptly disconnected the call.

Clara stared at her phone, hardly believing what she had heard.

I've given everything I have to LABT. I've spent more time in the corps de ballet and covered for more sick and injured dancers than just about anyone on the roster. Doesn't any of that count for something?

She rubbed her temples. Like any other injury, all she could do was wait for her body to heal on its own.

I'll deal with LABT and Artum when I get back to LA. For now, I'm on vacation. Since I'm out indefinitely, I might as well extend it a couple of days. I deserve it. I've taken maybe ten days off total the last three years.

Chapter Fifteen

DAVID

In the early afternoon, David marched briskly at a pace that would impress any general of the British Army up to apartment 1A of Kensington Palace. He pounded on the front door with determination.

"Is the Prince of Wales awake yet?" he inquired impatiently.

"No, sir. Should he be? His diary was clear last we checked. Dr. Evans prescribed rest for today as the best medicine," responded Parker, the butler that had served on Eddie's staff since childhood.

"Unfortunately, Parker, there was an incident yesterday. I need him up for a chat before he sees his father." David frowned.

Resigned, the butler solemnly nodded. "Yes, sir."

David awaited Eddie in his gaming room. He paced the room to and fro, hands tucked behind his back, contemplating his next move.

What can I say to him that might make a difference this time? It's as if whatever I tell him goes in one ear and out the other.

The staff of Kensington Palace was well known for the efficient and discreet manner in which they worked. In no time at all, Eddie was awakened, dressed, and ushered into David's presence before he had time to process what was going on. He still relied on his staff to shuffle him from place to place, unless it had to do with playing polo or sports cars.

Eddie knocked on the door and entered. Apart from his bloodshot eyes, he appeared no worse for wear, dressed in a charcoal suit, navy tie, and white dress shirt. David stopped his pacing.

The cousins exchanged nods.

"Eddie."

"David." His cousin shuffled over to the sofa across from the fireplace.

"Remain standing. Eyes front," David ordered in a commanding tone he hadn't used since his army days.

Eddie gulped.

Like a shark, David circled him. "Let's take a step back in time to yesterday. I want you to have a good think. Consider every single thing you did from the moment you first awoke."

Eddie's nose wrinkled.

"Now look at me." David crossed his arms and stood with his feet planted apart. "Do you recall where it all went wrong?"

"No." Eddie lowered his chin and stared intently at the carpet.

"Allow me to refresh your memory. Two days ago, you rang me while I was in America and told me there was an emergency. I rushed back home to find that the so-called emergency was you overreacting to being dumped. Is it starting to come back to you now?"

Eddie's face drained of color. "There's still a few gaps in my memory, but I remember being sick, then waking up here."

"A few gaps in your memory?" David pinched the bridge of his nose. "You are the Prince of Wales, the future king and head of state. What type of example or message does that send to the rest of the world?"

Eddie continued to stare at the ground.

"I've used every way imaginable to try and make you understand what an incredible privilege it is to be born into this family. You have the opportunity to make a real difference in the world, yet here you are instead, choosing to squander it away." David threw his hands up into the air. "If you wish to continue the path that you're on, by all means, go right ahead. You're an adult. You're old enough to understand that every choice you make comes with consequences. From here on out, I'm finished cleaning up your messes."

David leaned against Eddie's favorite recliner. "Your father's asked me let you know that when you meet with him in an hour, you will have an important decision to make."

Eddie slowly raised his chin, meeting his cousin's gaze. "What decision?"

"You'll have to choose whether you'll remain the Prince of Wales, or if you will resign from your position and step back from royal life. The choice is yours."

It's a lot to ask of him, but Uncle Reg is right. He has to decide on his own terms what his future is going to look like.

"I could be plain old Eddie Wales. No more media. No more spotlights."

"Yes, you could."

Eddie stood taller, opening and closing his mouth.

"There was a woman last night too, wasn't there?" He stumbled over to the sofa and sank down onto it. "I crashed into her on the way to the loo. It's all starting to come back to me now."

David rubbed his forehead "She's a ballerina. You injured her foot."

"I never intended for anyone to get hurt." His blue eyes swam with guilt.

"I know you didn't, but it's too late to change that. It's already happened."

"I need to find her and apologize." Eddie's shoulders hunched.

"You can take care of that after you meet with your father."

His cousin went rigid. "He's going to kill me! What am I going to tell him? What am I going to do?"

David stood and walked over to Eddie. "You'll face him like an adult and the soldier you're about to become. Own your mistakes and inform him what your choice is going to be."

Eddie held his head in his hands. "I don't know if I can."

"You'll find a way." David patted his hand.

"What if I make the wrong choice?"

He placed a hand on Eddie's shoulder. "You're still my cousin. No matter what you decide, I'll still be here for you."

Silence filled the room.

David cleared his throat. *Time to play my trick card.*

"You know, when I was in America, there was one project I was working on that wasn't tied to any state business."

Eddie's head shot up. "What were you doing?" he asked slowly.

"I was working on securing the last couple of investors we needed to launch our charitable foundation."

"You mean the kids in the children's wing at St. Mary's Hospital will finally be able to have those art and music classes?"

"Yes."

Eddie wrapped his arms around David. "They're going to be so excited when I see them."

"I hate to break it to you, but I doubt they'd remember you."

Eddie broke away. "I visit them every week, they wouldn't forget me that quickly."

It was David's turn to be surprised. "Every week?"

"Yeah. I go on Sunday nights. It's less busy. I like to keep the visits quiet, so it doesn't stress the children out too much."

Perhaps there's hope for you yet.

Chapter Sixteen
CLARA

LATER THAT AFTERNOON

Clara: Are you back in LA now?

Amanda: We're about three hours away from landing, somewhere over the Midwest. I'm sooooooooooooo tired. It's been the longest two days ever. I can't wait to curl up in my bed and take a long siesta.

Clara: Do you have time to talk?

Amanda: For you, always! How's London? And how'd last night go?

Clara: Do you want the short version or the long version?

Three dots blinked. Amanda was typing.

Amanda: Short. I'm only on crew rest for another twenty minutes.

Clara: Crew rest is for sleeping. I can text you later.

Amanda: I napped for a whole hour. Besides, if I fall asleep now, I won't want to get up again. So spill the tea.

Clara: My life has turned into a weird Disney slash Hallmark movie.

Amanda: ???

Clara: Problems with your airline and my hotel booking put me on a literal collision course with royalty. And now, I'm sitting in my hotel room with a cast on my foot debating on messaging Prince David about lunch tomorrow.

Amanda: SHUT THE FRONT DOOR! MY BRAIN IS ABOUT TO IMPLODE! ROYALTY?! A CAST?! I NEED THE FULL STORY THE SECOND I LAND!

Clara: *Nodding emoji*

Amanda: First off, are you okay?

Clara: I've been better, but I'm holding on.

Amanda: Do you want me to hop on the first plane to London? I can be there in fifteen hours.

Clara: I can't do that to you. You've literally just worked two long back-to-back flights.

Amanda: The job of a bestie is to be there for your bestie. If you need me, I'll be there. No ifs, ands, or buts.

Clara: I can manage.

Amanda: Just promise me if anything changes, you'll let me know ASAP.

Clara: I promise.

Amanda: Okay. Now that that's sorted out, text your prince and set up that lunch date! Don't wait.

Clara: I don't know.

Amanda: I can totally see him as being your type. Prince David is known for being kind of an introvert. He tends to shy away from the spotlight. The press calls him the "Boring Royal" because of it, but in actuality, he's probably the most active member of the entire royal family.

Clara: Good to know. Anything else I should be aware of?

Amanda: It's no fun if I just tell you stuff. Have lunch with him and find out exactly what type of man he is. *Winking emoji*

Three dots blinked.

Amanda: And if you bump into Prince Edmund, I'll love you forever if you happen to set me up on a date with him.

Clara: *Rolling eyes emoji*

Amanda: I know. I'm a ham. I'll call you the second I land. I heart you.

Clara: Ditto.

Five Minutes Later

Clara: Hello, Your Royal Highness. I realize I probably should've been using your official title earlier. Sorry about that. When we spoke this morning, you said your agenda was wide open. How does tomorrow look for lunch?

The ball is in your court, sir.

Ten Minutes Later

David: It's David. Not YRH. Not HRH. Not Prince. Not Duke. Not even Leeds. David. Lunch sounds perfect. Would you like me to arrange the details?

Clara: I'm sorry, David. I wasn't sure. And yes, please. I don't know the city very well.

David: Would eleven be too early to meet?

Clara: I don't have any plans, so anytime is fine.

David: Brilliant. I'll see you then. In the meantime, why not have Michael take you to a show on the West End?

Clara: West End?

David: Think Broadway.

Clara: Oh, any recommendations?

David: *Hamilton, The Lion King,* or *Six.*

Clara: Got it. I'll look them up now.

David: Have fun!

Grinning madly at her phone, Clara wondered how it was so easy to text a man she still knew practically nothing about. This morning, she'd intended to keep their relationship strictly professional, but once they'd started chatting, she'd found herself intrigued and saddened when their conversation was over. There was something about him that attracted her in a way she'd never been drawn to a man before.

Chapter Seventeen
CLARA

The next afternoon, a black Range Rover sped along the driveway leading up from the main road to a palace. Clara's eyes widened at the sight of the imposing red bricks, many glass windows, and a perfectly manicured lawn.

Her stomach somersaulted. "Which palace is this?"

"Kensington Palace. This is one of the oldest royal residences, dating back to William and Mary in 1689," Michael offered. "Did Leeds mention where he lives?"

"No, he never told me." The car entered into a small courtyard, and Michael parked it and turned off the motor. Her eyes roamed, taking in foliage and a small fountain. "I mean, I figured a prince would live in a palace, but thinking about it and seeing it in the flesh are two very different things."

"I understand where you're coming from. It was a bit of an adjustment when I first came to work for Leeds too. I never pictured myself driving his car about London, but here I am," Michel mused.

"What were your plans before you met him?"

"I always thought I'd spend my entire working life in the army, but once I'd served under Captain Leeds's command for two years, he'd earned my respect."

"You're not going to tell me what he did to earn your respect, are you?"

"Another story for another ride, miss." Michael's lips twisted. "Here we are. Apartments 1A and 1B. Let me pop around and assist you."

Clara positioned herself as the car door opened, careful to resist the urge to step down. Michael held the crutches out and offered his arm to her. The more practice she got in, the better. He let her do most of the maneuvering until she was ready to move.

"Thanks, Michael."

"All part of the job, Miss Little." He closed the car door and indicated Clara should follow him.

Stairs. The enemy. At least they're not too steep.

"If you take my left arm and use the rail, it might be a bit easier."

The door to the apartment clicked open. David rushed down toward her. Today, he wore fitted dove-gray trousers and blue button-up shirt. How should she greet him?

He laughed. "Welcome to my flat."

"It doesn't look very flat?"

His eyes sparkled in amusement. "A flat is the term we use for an apartment in the UK."

She inclined her head. "I should've known."

He ran a hand through his hair. "I thought for today we might keep it a bit casual and have a picnic out of my kitchen. I'd planned to take you out for a traditional English picnic, but the weather had other ideas."

They both glanced at the darkened sky covered with thick, heavy clouds. Small droplets of water fell onto their shoulders.

"Let's get you out of the rain." His forehead creased. "Do you mind being carried up the steps? It might be a little easier than hopping up."

Her heart beat a little faster, and her breath hitched. Clara looked over to Michael, who stood back, giving them some privacy.

"If it's the fastest way."

"Leave the crutches here. I'll return for them in a moment."

Placing an arm under her legs and another around her back, he scooped her to his chest. She was once again greeted with a woody scent. It was clean and masculine. The lightweight fabric of his shirt brushed against her cheek. It was linen, just like the lining of his suit jacket.

Once inside, David carried her through a hallway with black-and-white-checkered floors and deposited her on a chair in his kitchen. A wicker basket sat atop a quartz marble countertop. She'd expected it to be sleek and ultramodern, but instead it was homey. The cabinets were made from rich oak, and plants sat on the windowsills. Two floating shelves contained a small selection of cookbooks with colorful sticky-note flags poking out of the top.

"Nice kitchen. No on-call chef?" she joked.

David ran a ran a hand through his hair. "Eddie has a chef, but not me. I prefer to fend for myself."

"David, is she here?" A man with slouched posture appeared in the doorway. His eyes widened at seeing Clara. He reminded her of a young schoolboy. He had a lanky six-foot frame, and sandy-blonde hair and vibrant green eyes.

"Clara, please meet my cousin Edmund. Most people call him Eddie, though."

Seeing the two cousins stand side-by-side, she noticed they shared a number of physical similarities, but Eddie was much leaner than David and built like a long-distance runner.

Slowly lifting his chin to meet her gaze, he extended his hand and spoke softly. "Miss Little, I want to offer you my sincerest apology for my behavior toward you. I promise I will do whatever is in my power to try and make it up to you. I've spent the last twenty-four hours soul searching, and I promise you that I won't ever let something like that happen again." The words tumbled out of his mouth, his eyes burning with passion as he spoke.

I can tell he genuinely means that. I should be angry and resentful at him, but I can't be. Life is too short to hold grudges. He looks so much like a kid who's aware he's majorly screwed up, and from here on out will do his best to be a better person. If our encounter turns his life around, then actually, if it had to happen, I'm glad it was with me.

"Apology accepted," Clara responded without missing a beat.

"Thank you, Miss Little. I know you didn't have to, but thank you," Eddie said, releasing a deep breath. His shoulders relaxed somewhat, but he still stood guarded. "It it's all right with the two of you, I'll just be heading back over to my flat before I leave for the shelter."

David nodded. "I'll touch base with you later tonight."

Clara held up her hand. "Bye, Eddie. It was nice to meet you."

He waved meekly and departed.

Once the front door clicked closed, David busied himself moving about the kitchen, pulling out plates, cutlery, and glasses. "As cross as I am with him, I'm also impressed with how he's handling himself. Maybe he will be ready for Sandhurst in a couple months. I heard from my uncle this morning that Eddie stayed up half the night writing up a plan of action of how he could start 'reforming' himself, as he called it. His first order of business is going to be to spend the afternoon volunteering at a shelter for displaced people."

Clara was learning to appreciate David's gentle soul. She was drawn in by his compassion and concern over his cousin.

"He's only just realized what adulting means, hasn't he?" she remarked, resting her hands on the table. "How old is he?"

"I certainly hope so." David sighed. "He's twenty, almost twenty-one."

"Does Eddie have any siblings? What about you?"

"You don't know?" He faced her, blinking slowly.

"If I did, I wouldn't be asking." She raised an eyebrow. "I've heard your names before, of course, but I didn't see any reason to care about what your family is up to. I've always been laser-focused on my dance career." She winced. "That sounds terrible when I say it out loud."

I'll leave out the part about Amanda's huge crush on Eddie. David doesn't need to think I'm any stranger than I already am.

"It's rare, but also incredibly refreshing to hear." His eyes crinkled. "Eddie has a younger sister named Alice. As for me, I'm an only child. How about yourself?"

"I'm an only child." She stared off at a plant. "I don't know if I have any biological siblings; I was adopted when I was two."

She always found it challenging to discuss her family.

She never wanted to be treated with sympathy once people learned she was adopted. She'd been lucky to have a set of parents who loved her, and in the end, that was all that truly mattered.

Picking up on her mood, David changed the subject. He lifted open the lid of the basket, removing container after container of food. "I wasn't sure about your food preferences, so I picked up a little bit of everything from the market. I have bread, meats, salad, fresh vegetables, crackers, cheeses, crisps, and a few other odds and ends. I hope this will work for you."

"Definitely. The spread looks amazing! There are so many yummy options." She scooted forward in her seat. "I can eat anything except shellfish. I'm allergic to them." She picked up a plate and started filling it.

As they ate, their conversation started to flow. She'd worried she might not have much in common with a royal, but as she was finding out, he did many of the same things a normal person did. Despite having a security detail for major outings, he didn't keep a household staff, and he preferred to do his own grocery shopping.

David pushed his plate aside. "You're more of a workaholic than I am! I can't even imagine waking up, spending all day rehearsing, having a dinner break, then returning to the theatre later that night for a performance."

"It *is* a difficult lifestyle, I'll give you that. But I've always known that my career won't last forever. Most dancers retire by the time they hit their thirties. I'm hoping I'll be able to stay healthy enough to make it that far." Her cheeks burned. "Theoretically, now that I'm a soloist, I won't have to dance every night anymore like I did when I was in the corps deballet."

"Having that thing on your foot must be pure torture,

then." His gaze traveled to her cast. "How are you going to get by for the next couple of weeks?"

"I'm trying to look at it from the perspective that for the first time in a long time, my body is going to be able to fully rest. Besides my foot, I have some injuries from overuse that will have a chance to heal." She rubbed the back of her neck. "On the flip side, my friend Amanda was joking that maybe I'll actually discover how to have a proper work-life balance. My extended layoff is giving me a chance to do things I never normally would."

"Such as?"

She counted on her fingers. "Take a vacation, pick up a new hobby, catch up on the massive pile of book-of-the-month club books I subscribe to and just leave sitting in their shipping envelopes." She shrugged. "Who knows, maybe I'll even sign up for a dating app for something."

A funny expression crossed David's face, disappearing as quickly as it had appeared. Clara didn't think much of it.

"I hope you'll consider extending you stay in London a few days and turn it into that vacation you've been looking to take."

"I'd meant to ask whether you'd mind if I stayed at the St. George a little while longer. I know that it's a luxury hotel—"

He held up his hand. "I *insist* you stay for as long as you'd like. Three weeks, six months, a year... it doesn't make any difference to me."

"Thank you."

Pushing his chair back, David stood up, collected the dishes, and set them in the sink. "What show did you end up seeing on the West End yesterday?"

"*Hamilton*! I totally understand what all the hype's about now. The music and songs were out of this world.

It's such a three-sixty from what I'm used to." She pivoted in her chair to face him, enjoying the sight of him unbuttoning the cuffs of his dress shirt and rolling up the ends to his elbows. "I might have to see another show before I leave London."

"I'm happy you had a brilliant time." He added some soap to a yellow sponge. "Have you made any plans to do some sightseeing?"

"Nothing fixed, but if Michael doesn't mind, I was thinking of asking him to drop me off at the British Museum. I've done a little research, and I think I might also try squeezing in the National Gallery, and maybe even catch the Changing of the Guard ceremony." She drummed her fingers on the table. "The only question is, how much walking am I going to be able to handle?"

Turning on the tap, he slowly lathered a plate. "If you'll hold off on the Changing of the Guard, I can arrange for you to watch it from a place where you can sit."

"Oh wow, thanks."

"I also had a thought about you getting around that doesn't involve using crutches." She perked up with interest. "Would you be open using a wheelchair and letting me show you some of the city's sights?"

She blinked slowly. "I'm open to it, but what about all the logistics? Doesn't that involve having a security detail with you? And what about your work? I don't want to take you away from anything important."

"Leave all that to me. I'm a master multitasker."

"Another skill you've picked up by watching *Sherlock?*"

He turned and winked, then focused on the dishes.

Waves of excitement shot through her body. He was so different than any other man she'd ever been around, not that she had much of a dating history to go by. Normally, she lived vicariously through Amanda.

Wait, this isn't really a date. It's just lunch. We're just two people having a meal together, chatting about life. There isn't anything else going on. At least I don't think there is. She gulped. She couldn't be falling for a man she'd only known three days. Could she?

Chapter Eighteen
CLARA

The next morning, David and Clara took their time meandering through the galleries of the British Museum, enjoying the exhibits. His security team —George and another protection officer—discreetly posed as tourists, never far from them.

The actual tourists ignored them, more interested in selfies and seeing art. Clara had to hand it to David. Attempting to be as non-descript as possible, he'd dressed in a navy button-up shirt, a baseball cap, sneakers, and dark-wash jeans. He gave off a Clark Kent vibe in his glasses. A superhero in disguise.

She'd thought he was sharply dressed in a suit, but the casual look agreed with him too. If stood next to one of the Greek and Roman statues, he would have no trouble fitting in.

"There are over eight million objects in the museum's collection. We won't be able to see everything, but have a look over the map, and we'll try to hit the exhibits that catch your eye," he said as he pushed Clara's wheelchair. She opened the paper and spread it across her lap.

David wasn't kidding—this was one of the largest museums she'd ever been to. Where should they even start? Her head started to spin. "You know what, forget the map. Let's just wander around. Sometimes the best surprises are the ones that are unplanned."

They moved at a leisurely pace around the ground floor, passing through the Egyptian and Assyrian antiquities, until Gallery 4, where three large tour groups stood unaware of their surroundings. They pushed past one another and jockeyed to get as close as they could to the glass case containing the Rosetta Stone.

"There are three scripts on the tablet—hieroglyphics, Demotic, and Ancient Greek," David whispered into her ear. "I'm always in awe that the discovery of this single item managed to unlock all the mysteries of ancient Egypt to the world."

As the groups began to clear out, they moved up to the display.

"Wow. The carvings are so intricate." She snapped a photo with her phone. "The edges look chipped. I wonder when that happened?"

"The Rosetta Stone is actually a part of a larger block. It was discovered broken."

The next wave of tourists entered the room, and David pushed Clara out of the way before they were swarmed. Nestled safely in a corner, they faced one another. "You're impressing me with all this knowledge," she said.

"I did a little research last night." He removed his hat to scratch his head, then began pushing her toward the ancient Greek and Roman galleries. "I have a decent memory for names and dates. It's one of the reasons I studied history as an undergraduate at Oxford."

Clara let out a low whistle. "Oxford."

David stopped the wheelchair and looked at her. "It's not as impressive as being a professional ballerina. There are far more Oxford grads than dancers of your caliber."

"I appreciate you saying that, but I respectfully disagree."

He laughed. "We'll agree to disagree."

"Did anyone ever tell you that you're gifted at being able to think on the fly of just the right thing to say? Maybe you should've been a lawyer," she joked.

"Becoming a barrister *was* something that I considered at one point," he admitted.

"And you didn't because…?"

"Because as a teenager, I was painfully shy, and my uncle decided I'd be better served by doing an officer course at Sandhurst and joining the army."

She tried to picture him in a scarlet tunic and massive black hat, marching forward with a sword held high. She wrinkled her nose.

"What are you thinking?"

She caught him watching her closely. "I can't see you as the type to bark orders. You're very soft-spoken and easygoing."

"I assure you, I can," David joked. "George and Michael can attest to it."

He unlocked the brakes of the wheelchair. "Are you ready to get going again?"

She nodded. The next gallery, number 18, featured artifacts from ancient Greece. They walked past several cases filled with shimmering gold coins and terra-cotta pottery.

"How heavy is the black hat the soldiers wear when they guard the palace?" Clara asked.

"The bearskin cap? It's heavy, but not quite as heavy as a cavalry helmet."

She glanced behind her. "Help a girl out. You were in the cavalry?"

"Uh-huh. I was a captain of the Life Guards, one of the two Household Cavalry Mounted Regiment's divisions. Think horses, red tunics, and gold helmets with white plumes."

That, I can absolutely picture. He'd look so majestic on a horse.

"How long did you serve for?"

"Four years. I wish it were longer, but my uncle asked me to step in and become a working royal. He reminded me that by representing the crown, I am still serving my country, just in a different way."

"And your uncle is a man you don't say no to."

"Exactly."

The air was suddenly filled with the scent of fresh coffee. David stopped pushing her. They both took a sniff and exchanged glances.

"Coffee break," they said at the same time, and laughed.

He stopped right outside the café. "How do you take your coffee?"

"I'll take it with two sugars and room for a little milk."

"I'll be right back."

Clara was happy to have a moment to herself. She watched the other tourists sit down at tables nearby, glued to their phones. She shook her head. Even on vacation, some people couldn't find a way to unplug themselves and step away from social media.

I haven't had this much time on my hands ever. If I were in LA, I'd be at home sitting on the sofa, thinking about what the company was doing in rehearsal. I'd be making myself miserable. But being here, it's like I'm in a different world. I haven't thought about dance once today, until now. David's working his magic on me.

He returned a couple of minutes later with two steaming cups of coffee, a blueberry muffin, a chocolate chip cookie, and a snickerdoodle. They made their way to a private members' room on the first floor, where they had the space to themselves. It was much quieter.

"I don't know about you, but I can't have coffee without something sweet." David sat down at a table across from Clara. "I couldn't decide what I wanted, so I got the muffin and the cookies. You can have first pick, or we can share."

Her eyes fluttered. "If it's a choice between chocolate and anything else, the chocolate always wins."

He slid the plate toward her. "It's yours, then. Do you think that you'll want any of the muffin or the other cookie?"

She shook her head and pulled the chocolate chip cookie closer to her. "Nope. This is all I need." He was too good to be true. Chocolate and coffee. Two of her favorite things in life.

He rubbed his hands together. "Then don't mind me—I'm about to devour the muffin."

"Be my guest."

Clara took a sip of her coffee. The more time she spent with David, the more she was learning she should never judge a book by its cover.

"So this best friend you keep referencing—can you tell me a little more about her?"

"Her name's Amanda Collins, and once you meet her, you'll never forget her. She's got a larger-than-life personality," Clara said, breaking off a piece of her cookie. "We've been besties for about ten years. We're both from Seattle."

David chewed thoughtfully. "Did you meet in school?"

"In a way." She swallowed hard as memories of the past began to resurface. "My dad was friends with her dad. There was an accident and my parents"—her voice trembled—"they didn't make it." A stray tear welled in the corner of her eye. "Mr. and Mrs. Collins took me in and have always treated me like their own daughter."

David pushed his food and coffee aside and reached for her hand. "Forget I ever asked."

"No," she said, her voice steadier. "It's been a long time. My therapist has always pushed me to be open and talk to others about them. She said sharing their stories helps keep their memories alive and would help me process my own thoughts and emotions."

He squeezed her hand, offering her comfort. Another salty tear leaked out of her eye, then another. She took a deep breath, allowing the release.

"Mom always wanted to be a dancer, like me, but her parents didn't see it as a viable career option. She used to joke that the real reason she signed me up for the Mommy and Me dance classes as a kid was so she could dance too." Clara chuckled.

"When I told Mom and Dad that I wanted to be a become a professional ballerina, they were so supportive. Dad would spend his days off building me a little studio in the garden shed. Mom took sewing lessons to figure out how to make me a tutu. Costumes don't come cheap."

David rubbed circles on her hand, giving Clara his full and undivided attention as she gave a glimpse into her childhood.

I'd normally never share things like this with anyone except Amanda. She's my person. The one who knows all my deepest and darkest secrets. My hopes and my desires. David's a stranger, but something inside is telling me that I can trust him. I always trust my instincts.

~

"Thank you for telling me about your parents. They sound like they were wonderful people," David said in a hushed tone when she was finished reminiscing. He had moved his chair, so he was right beside her, still holding her hand, caressing her wrist gently with his thumb.

"They were," she sniffled. Her body was no longer wracked with sobs.

"I haven't known you very long," he said, his blue eyes sparkling with raw emotion, like diamonds, "but I'd wager that if your mum and dad were here right now, they'd be so proud of you for not only following your dreams, but also for the person you've become."

"You really think so?"

"Yes, I do." He nodded emphatically. "You are kind, compassionate, and you have a beautiful heart. Not just anybody would've helped me out at the airport when I couldn't find my wallet."

Instinctually, she raised her arms. David leaned forward and wrapped her in a warm embrace. Clara squeezed him tightly, inhaling and exhaling deeply, feeling a release from the sadness she'd carried with her earlier.

"Thanks for listening to me." As they pulled away, she wiped her eyes with the back of her hand. "I'm sorry for going all emo on you. I'm sure it's not what you expected today to turn into."

"Don't ever apologize for having a cry. And while we're on the topic I want you to know that I—"

Suddenly, a cool female's voice announced over a speaker, "The museum will be closing in fifteen minutes. All visitors should please begin making their way to the exits."

David and Clara jumped.

"It's four in the afternoon already? I can't believe we've been here all day." She opened and closed her mouth. Her body felt heavy, and all her muscles ached. She wasn't used to sitting for so long. "Now, what were you saying before you were cut off?"

His Adam's apple bobbed up and down. "Just that I'm—"

A door opened. They turned to see George entering. "Leeds, are you and Miss Little just about ready to depart? I'm supposed to remind you that your mother is expecting you for dinner at six tonight."

His shoulders heaved. He let out a deep sigh. Their private moment together was over.

"Tonight's Thursday, isn't it?" David stroked his jaw. "I dine with Mum every Thursday," he told her.

"I've monopolized you enough today. With traffic, it's going to take a while to head back to the St. George," Clara said, trying to downplay her disappointment. She was burning with curiosity to know what David had tried to tell her before they were interrupted.

"I suppose you're right." He stood and walked behind Clara to push her to the door. "We're ready, George."

As they departed the museum through the main hallway, she reflected on their time together. She focused on the way his hair was out of place when he removed his hat, and how the corners of his mouth curved up when he was happy. When he touched her hand and held it the entire time she spoke to him about her parents, it was a warm and comforting presence. Pangs of sadness hit her. She didn't know when she'd be able to see him next.

∼

Later that evening, Amanda nearly broke Clara's eardrums when she screamed into the phone. "You spent *all* day with Prince David? That's like an official date! My bestie is dating royalty!" she gushed.

"It wasn't a date." Clara pinched the bridge of her nose. She replayed the entire time at the museum in her head for the millionth time.

"It so was a date!" Amanda shouted. Clara held the phone an inch from her ear. "Give me details! What was he wearing? What's he like?"

"He was casual today in jeans and a button-up. And he's…" She searched for the right words. "Real."

"That's not enough for me to go on. I need more. How was he real?"

"I don't know. . ." Clara huffed. "He may be a self-proclaimed workaholic, but he's also incredibly aware of everything that's going on around him. He's smart, funny, patient, organized, and…"

"Oh, C, I can hear it in your voice. As Ariel's older sisters said in *The Little Mermaid*, you've got it bad."

She frowned, trying to recount the scene Amanda was referencing. "What do I have?"

Amanda giggled. "That's what King Triton said."

"Amanda."

"You're. Falling. For. Him."

"No, that's not possible." Her eyes widened. She fell back against the silky pillows of the bed. "He's practically a stranger. A girl doesn't start falling for a guy after three days."

"That's not how it's coming across to me," Amanda said, raising her voice again.

"Okay, I'll admit, I *like* the man, but I wouldn't go as far as saying that I'm falling for him." Clara set the phone down and stared up at the soft glow of the chandelier above the four-poster bed.

Yet.

"Suit yourself. I call it like I see it, C." She heard the sound of her friend unzipping her suitcase.

"Have you met my future husband, Prince Edmund, yet? He's only four years younger than me, you know. He would be my perfect match, I just know it. Maybe you could arrange for us to have a double date."

Clara snickered. Amanda had held a crush on Eddie for as long as she'd known her. She still had the cardboard cutout of him that she'd had in her childhood room. Clara just wasn't supposed to know that it lived in Amanda's spare-bedroom closet.

"Yes, I've met him, and a hard pass on the double date. I have no idea when or if I'm even going to see David again."

Amanda squealed once more. "When. Did. You. Meet. Edmund?"

Clara's face fell. Her bestie wasn't quite up to speed on the full story yet. "How much unpacking do you have left to do?"

"Enough."

Her eyes fluttered. "Let's start back at the beginning…"

Chapter Nineteen

CLARA

A week passed. David continued to serve as Clara's official London tour guide. Together, they explored Greenwich, the Tower of London, and the Victoria and Albert Museum, and sailed on a Thames River cruise. Clara couldn't believe just how much ground she had covered. She was also becoming much more proficient at using crutches. Now she was on her way to the next item on her list.

Michael twisted and checked on his charge in the back seat as they waited to pass through security. "Are you feeling all right, Miss Little? It's not like you to be so quiet."

Smoothing down the fabric of her skirt, she replied drily, "When David spoke to me about having a VIP viewing of the Changing of the Guard ceremony, I thought I might have a spot near the front of the gate where I could watch it. I never imagined he'd arrange for me to be a guest at Buckingham Palace. Do you realize who lives here?"

A policeman finished checking the underside of the car. "You're all clear."

"Thanks. Cheers, Joe," Michael said.

The car advanced down a long drive shaded by trees.

"Yes, miss," the driver replied calmly. "Leeds's maternal family resides here, but you shouldn't worry. I doubt you'll cross paths with the king or queen today."

Her hands shook. The imposing building she'd driven past on her first day in London grew larger. "Do you think I dressed appropriately?" She pulled the fabric over her knees. "This was the only dress I had."

Thank goodness my luggage actually turned up, or else I might not even have a dress! Did I ever tell David thank you for his help in tracking it down?

"Miss Little, breathe. Your attire is just right." The car came to a stop. Michael assisted Clara out of the car and waited patiently until she had steadied herself on the crutches. "Leeds sent a message along a little earlier, that he was running a tad behind schedule. You'll have a backup guide today until he can join you."

Clara's stomach performed summersaults. "Who would that be?"

"Me." Eddie leaned casually against the pillar by the door, waiting for her with his hands in his pockets, appearing much more relaxed and in his element. He was dressed in a pair of gray slacks and a crisp white dress shirt. His eyes were clearer, and brightened in excitement at seeing Clara. "I know I'm not your favorite person, but I hoped to have a couple of minutes to chat with you."

Still in shock, she bobbed her head up and down.

"Your Royal Highness, I leave Miss Little in your hands."

"Thanks, Michael."

Should she curtsy? Or bow? Could she speak to him?

Or should she let him initiate the conversation? Technically, they'd met at David's flat, but this was different. They were at Buckingham Palace, and Eddie was the heir to the throne.

"I don't bite, you know."

Finding her voice, she managed, "It's nice to see you again, Edmund."

"Please." He waved her off. "You've seen me at my worst. It's Eddie." He cleared his throat. "I hope you're doing well. I'm sorry once again for"—he gestured to the cast—"that."

"Eddie, I already accepted your apologies. Don't look so stressed. Please, it almost hurts me to see you so down."

"Thank you," he said, looking up.

"David mentioned that you've been fitting quite a few engagements into your schedule," she said. "He was concerned you might be pushing yourself too hard."

He also mentioned that you've been avoiding him.

"David's too good to me." Eddie rubbed the back of his neck. "Let him know that I promise I can handle it. From now until I join the army, I'm fully committed to showing my father and the family that I can carry my own weight as a working royal."

Eddie led her down the hall to a service elevator. He let out a deep breath and didn't speak until the doors opened. A wheelchair sat outside of it. "It's a bit of a walk. David thought you might be more comfortable with the wheelchair."

She took a seat and handed her crutches to Eddie, who placed them on the back of the chair. Silence passed between them for another minute as Clara took in her surroundings. She'd seen photos of some of the palace rooms in her guidebook. It was surreal to be inside, walking past them.

Clara stared at everything, from the red and gold carpets to the elaborate glass chandeliers. The room closest to the elevator exit contained a large portrait of the late queen. Clara studied her face, looking for any resemblance to David.

Eddie remained silent. She needed to lighten the mood. "David's staff has been trying hard to sell to me that he's an amazing boss. I've heard more times than I can count that he's a 'good bloke.' That's all well and good, but I want to know that he has flaws just like the rest of us. Do you have any embarrassing stories you'd be willing to share with me about your cousin?"

Eddie stopped pushing the chair and looked down at Clara. She turned to find him staring at her with an eyebrow raised. "Only if you promise never to tell him who your source was."

She made the gesture of zipping her lips closed. "Scout's honor."

"Off the top of my head, I have two memories," Eddie said with a mischievous glint in his eyes. "The first one was on the night my sister Alice turned ten and was invited to attend her first State Ball. David was with her in the middle of the dance floor when the seam of his trousers split on his bum, revealing a pair of bright red boxer briefs." Eddie started laughing. "David tried to use Alice's skirt to hide behind, but my sister was oblivious. She kept shouting at him to let go of her skirt. It ended up only bringing more attention to him. Father finally took note of what was going on and took pity on him by cutting in to finish the dance with Alice. Only then was he able to slip away."

"Oh no!" Clara's body shook with laughter. "A State

Dinner too? Ouch. Poor David." She wiped a small tear from the corner of her eye. "I'm almost afraid to ask what your other memory is."

"When I was about thirteen, David invited me over for a lad night at his flat. We watched films, played video games, and sang some awful karaoke. When it was time for dinner, I was extra excited. It was the first time I'd ever been allowed to order takeaway food. I'd heard my protection officers talking up Indian food, so that's what I decided to order."

"Uh-huh."

"I think I ended up ordering one of everything on the menu, but David being David was a good sport about it. When the food arrived, we each picked a container at random to try. I ended up with naan and David a curry. After he took about two bites of the food, his face turned a fiery red. He shot up from the table and darted around the guest bedroom shouting, "Hot!" In a moment of panic, I handed him the closest thing to me with water. He drank about half of it before he realized it was water from his fishbowl. The look on his face was priceless."

Both of them chuckled.

Eddie sighed. "With David, what you see is what you get. He rarely loses his temper and is one of the most easygoing gents out there. He's my best mate, and the brother I always wanted but never had."

"Thanks for sharing those stories with me."

A cool breeze hit Clara's face. The sounds of boots hitting the ground in unison and music filled the air. Eddie wheeled her out a side door onto a terrace under a covered arch. One company of soldiers in the famed scarlet tunics was lined up in two neat rows, while another company was in the process of marching through the palace's black-and-gold front gates.

"We'll watch the ceremony from here. I discovered this spot by accident as a child."

Looking out, it was a sea of people pressed shoulder to shoulder, watching the guards' every movement.

"Eddie, what if they see you?"

He puffed out his chest. "They won't. Trust me."

At eleven, after the Household Cavalry soldiers had ridden past, Eddie and Clara were heading inside when they encountered an elegantly dressed woman in a green blazer, her reddish hair secured in a low chignon. Despite the clash in colors, the woman pulled off the outfit flawlessly.

"Edmund! Well, if this isn't a fun surprise."

"Aunt Charlotte!" Eddie sputtered.

Clara inclined her head. "Your Royal Highness." She'd remembered being presented to the Princess Royal shortly before the gala began.

Princess Charlotte's brown eyes appraised Clara with a knowing smile. "Edmund, be a dear and bring Miss Little up to my sitting room. As it so happens, I've just asked my secretary, Abigail, to have a spot of tea brought up from the kitchens."

Clara could sense the waves of anxiety rolling off Eddie as he gripped the handles of her wheelchair tightly. "Yes, ma'am."

"Good lad."

Why was he so nervous around his aunt?

Turning, Princess Charlotte walked away with an air of importance, almost like a dancer. Clara wondered if she was a ballerina at one point in her life. Then she noticed the princess walked with her feet turned out.

I guess that answers my question. Old habits die hard.

"Eddie, you aren't going to leave me alone with your aunt, are you?" Clara whispered.

"If I stay, who's going to go get you backup?"

Clara, puzzled by his remark, watched Eddie make a hasty exit, leaving her to wonder just what he'd meant. With the aid of her crutches, she moved to a wooden chair positioned opposite an antique oak desk.

The room was bathed in natural light, offering a beautiful view of the palace gardens. The walls were a pale yellow. Two Degas ballerina portraits adorned the wall, immediately catching Clara's eye.

"Well, Miss Little, I must say, I hope you heal quickly. I thoroughly enjoyed your pas de deux last week. You left quite an impression with the dance community."

Clara turned her attention to Princess Charlotte, who was seated behind her desk.

"Thank you so much, Your Highness."

"You may call me Princess Charlotte."

The princess poured two cups of tea and offered a cup and saucer to her. "Thank you, ma'am."

She nodded. "And how are you enjoying London so far? Is it to your liking?"

"It's been a dream come true. I love the city and the people very much."

"Excellent." A coy smile appeared on Princess Charlotte's lips as she settled into her seat, crossing her legs at the ankle. "Can you envision yourself falling in love with London enough to contemplate a future here?"

Clara's hands trembled, causing hot amber liquid to spill over the cup's rim and onto the saucer. "Oh my," she said. Unfazed, the princess set her cup down and passed her a napkin. "Um… I don't know. If I had the right reason."

The princess picked up her cup once more. "It's not

public knowledge yet, but Evelyne Murdoch, one of the Westminster Ballet's principal dancers, will be retiring at the end of the season," she revealed, taking a sip. "I'm aware that Mr. Williamson has been keeping his eyes open for just the right person to fill that spot. She's one of Anton's most frequent partners. Judging from how well the pair of you worked together, I'm confident in saying that Mr. Williamson has added you to his short list of candidates."

Clara's pulse quickened as she hung on to the princess's every word. "Me? Short list?"

"Yes, dear," the princess said, her eyes narrowing. "Of course, Mr. Williamson is *not* in the habit of approaching dancers who are already under contract with other companies. Hypothetically speaking, however, if a *dancer* were to express an interest in auditioning for the company in the future, Mr. Williamson would be pleased to reach out to you when the timing was appropriate. Do you understand what I'm saying to you?"

I don't think she could be any more blunt. If I want to be considered for the spot, it'll be up to me to reach out to Mr. Williamson.

Clara considered how she could be diplomatic as possible. The Westminster Ballet was her dream company, but her loyalty was to Artum and LABT for taking a chance on her all those years ago.

"Ma'am, I understand perfectly well. I'm happy keep my options open. However, at the moment, my loyalty lies to LABT."

"I respect that."

As she reached over for her tea, the door to the princess's study abruptly banged open. David burst into the room, panting and disheveled. His hair was damp, his shirt was buttoned unevenly and wrinkled.

"David," both women admonished.

"Mum. Clara."

An alarm bell sounded in her head. Princess Charlotte was David's mother! Why hadn't she made the connection before?

Chapter Twenty

CLARA

"I'll pretend that you're attired appropriately and not as if you spent an evening at the pub," Princess Charlotte said. She pointed to her cheek, and David approached his mother and planted a kiss. "If you promise *not* to leave a wet mark on my sofa, you may sit. Otherwise, standing would be preferred. There's tea and biscuits on my desk."

"I'll stand."

Clara glanced from David to his mother. Seeing the pair of them together, she noted they had the same nose and facial structure, but that was all they seemed to share.

"Clara… er, Miss Little… hello," he greeted awkwardly with a wave.

"I was just about to ask Miss Little if she had any interest in attending the Westminster Ballet's performance of *Onegin* tomorrow evening as my guest."

David frowned. "Is that the event Abigail rang to ask if I could attend in your stead?"

"How silly of me. I must have forgotten that I'm otherwise engaged tomorrow." The princess placed a hand on her chest.

He rolled his eyes. Clara also found her claim hard to believe. Was the Princess Royal trying to play matchmaker? Even if David wasn't going, she'd still say yes. She'd never turn down an opportunity to attend the ballet.

"Princess Charlotte, I'd love to," she said.

"Excellent. I'll have my secretary arrange the details. David will escort you."

She tried to downplay her excitement by looking out the window at the gardens. "That sounds wonderful."

David rubbed his hands together. "Mother, I hate to interrupt your tea, but I promised Clara an extended tour of the grounds."

"Yes, yes. Of course." She assessed Clara, then her son. "Exploring the rose gardens might just take up your entire afternoon. I believe Reggie is out for a ride on Clover. You might even see him along the way. Enjoy."

David hastened over to assist Clara and settled her into the wheelchair. "It was nice meeting you, ma'am. Thank you for tea."

"You're most welcome." She winked. "I hope we'll have the privilege of seeing more of you."

David practically jogged out of the room, a spring in his step. Clara gripped the arms of the wheelchair tightly, her fingers turning white. "David, slow down."

"Can't. We need to clear out of Mum's area of the palace as quickly as possible."

"Why?"

"Because my mum is like Jane Austen's Emma. She's always playing matchmaker with me."

Clara giggled.

"You laugh, but it's true. She's attempted to set me up

on at least five or six blind dates over the last year alone. She won't stop until she has a crying grandchild in her arms."

Clara sighed. She could understand where the Princess Royal was coming from. All mothers wanted what was best for their children. From what Clara knew about David, he'd probably be happy to stay a bachelor without a little prodding from her.

She rearranged her hair so it was behind her. "If you don't feel up to attending the ballet with me, I won't ask you to. I don't want you to feel like you're stuck with me."

"That's exactly why I *want* to go. I *enjoy* spending time with you. I don't see tomorrow as a favor I'm doing for my mum; I'm choosing to spend the evening with a gorgeous and talented woman—you."

Clara's pulse raced. Hearing those magical words left her breathless.

"You're not such bad company yourself."

～

The water lilies in the Buckingham Palace ponds were said to rival that of Monet's home in Giverny. Clara couldn't imagine a more picturesque place to relax. There were delicate pink and white flowers atop the lily pads. The long branches of the willow trees swayed in the breeze, while songbirds sang melodic tunes.

"Is this canoe really sturdy enough to hold both of us?" Clara asked, eyeing the boat carefully. It creaked and dipped deep into the waterline as David settled in and located the oars.

"It's perfectly safe," he replied. "I've taken this canoe out hundreds of times with my cousins, and we haven't had too many problems. Trust me, this is the best way to enjoy the gardens. I want you to have the *full* experience."

She knew he was confident about the canoe and she shouldn't question him, but something didn't feel right. Should she say something or just go along with it? David was acting like an excited little boy. She didn't want to ruin his mood.

"If you're sure it's safe. I'm not the greatest swimmer." Clara bit her lip and followed him into the canoe.

His chest expanded. "Then it's a good thing that I just renewed my pool and water lifesaving certificate this morning. If anything happens, I can take care of us."

"Is that why you're dressed so sloppy?"

"Uh-huh. I was just about to pop into the shower when Eddie came running to find me. He was worried on my behalf about you being in Mum's care." He let out a throaty laugh. "I love my mother, but if you've never met her, she can be an intimidating woman."

"Your mother was fine. I was introduced before I danced last week. We chatted about ballet."

Should I mention anything to him about what the princess hinted to me? As amazing as it would be to even secure an audition with Westminster Ballet, I don't want to set myself up for disappointment if I try out and nothing comes from it. I've been put into that situation one too many times. Besides, even if I made his short list, Mr. Williamson might just end up deciding to promote a soloist from inside the company.

David pushed off from the small makeshift dock and rowed slowly around the perimeter of the pond. Clara let her guard down and relaxed. She watched the different birds swim around and a pair of swans glide off into the distance to a mound that looked like a nest.

"I picked up a few bread crusts if you feel like feeding the birds. Uncle doesn't particularly like it, but it's something my cousins and I do whenever we're out here."

"If it's a tradition, of course I want to do it. I haven't fed birds since I was a child. I appreciate watching them, but I'm not the biggest fan."

"I sense there is a story here." David smirked and took a handful of crumbs from the small picnic basket he had brought.

Clara shrugged. "Not much to tell. I was a child fascinated with swans. My mom took me to see *Swan Lake*, and I thought all swans were secretly princesses. One afternoon when we were at a park, I walked up to one and tried to pet it. Only instead of turning into a beautiful dancer, it bit me."

"You tried to pet a swan?"

Clara looked down into the water and skimmed her fingertips against the pond's surface. "Six-year-old me thought it was an awesome idea. I'm sure you had your share of dumb things you did when your parents weren't looking."

David grew quiet. "Mother and I have a close relationship now, but my parents weren't the most hands-on when I was a child. It was the nanny's responsibility to keep track of me."

Clara inhaled sharply.

"I'm ashamed to say that, yes, I often acted out. It was my way of trying to capture their attention. Eddie reminds me a lot of my younger self." He stopped rowing and let the oars hang loose. "The thing is, it's easy for me to sit here and judge them, but the adult me can understand that my parents were doing what they thought was right. They were raised with nannies too. Mum told me that when I was born, she was told by my nan that a child was to be seen, not heard."

She shivered. "It sounds so cold and informal."

"My nannies were kind people." David smiled sadly. "If there was one positive outcome, it was that Uncle Reg and Uncle Frank learned from how mum raised me to bring up my cousins according to more modern standards."

Clara placed her hands behind her and leaned back. She let the rays of the sun warm her face. "Can I ask about your dad? You don't mention him much."

He shrugged. "Mum and Dad married young and were ill-matched. They divorced the day I went off to boarding school when I was eight. We're not close. I think he spends most of his time in Spain these days."

"I'm sorry."

"Don't be. I came to terms with it long ago. My dad has my mobile number and knows how to reach me. We speak twice a year, on my birthday and around Christmastime. The more important thing is that I have loving relatives on Mum's side of the family and some excellent cousins."

Clara asked David about what it had been like attending a boarding school. He mentioned that the staff aimed to keep the students as busy as possible with sports, academics, and extracurricular activities so that there wasn't time to be lonely.

"I'm curious, what was it like for you attending a ballet school growing up?"

"Ballet was pretty much an after-school activity for me until I turned thirteen. Then I became a full-time student." Clara rubbed her hands over her forearms. "On a typical day, I had a morning class, followed by homeschool until lunch. At one, we'd start our afternoon classes and rehearsals."

He dipped the oar into the water. "I'm impressed by how committed you were."

"Unfortunately, ballet is a lot like gymnastics or figure skating. You have to decide at a young age if you want to make a career out of ballet. It takes years and years of training, and even then, there are no guarantees. There are way more dancers out there than professional contracts available."

"If your dancing didn't work out, what would you have done?"

"Funny you should ask. I would've applied to be a flight attendant like my bestie, Amanda. It nearly happened too. I had all the paperwork filed online and had an interview scheduled on the day I got the call to fly to LA for an audition."

"You're joking." His eyes widened.

"Afraid not." She picked at the fabric of her skirt. "After I graduated, it took me two years to get hired into a company. Between auditions, I was working as a barista, but the pay barely covered rent. I figured if I wasn't going to make it, I might as well have a job I at least was semi-passionate about."

"Was it for the travel benefits?"

"Yeah, it was." Clara nodded. "Amanda was always jet-setting around the globe, and I was jealous. Until this trip, I'd never traveled internationally before."

"Well, I'm certain that as soon as you're healed up, it won't be long before you're invited to the likes of Paris, Rome, Tokyo, and other places around the world."

She raised her head and looked at David. "You seem awfully sure of me."

He grinned. "It's all deductive reasoning."

They leaned in, holding one another's gazes. Her eyes

closed. Her breathing evened out. David dropped the oar and scooted closer to her. Brushing a lock of hair out of her face, he whispered, "You're so beautiful." His thumbs traced the outline of her lips. Their foreheads touched. But as David moved to kiss her, the canoe creaked and both he and Clara tumbled into the cold, scummy pond.

Chapter Twenty-One
DAVID

It took David a few moments to realize his stupid mistake. He scolded himself for not checking the canoe earlier as Clara had suggested.

Always listen to a woman's intuition.

He was a first-rate idiot for letting his pride get in the way. Clara was going to be livid when they got out of the water.

Using his long, powerful arms, he swam over to the capsized vessel and flipped it back over. He scanned the pond, hoping Clara would surface momentarily behind him. The pond wasn't particularly deep and had an average depth of about one and a half meters. He could touch the bottom with his toes.

Clara doggie paddled in his direction but was struggling to keep her head above water. Her limbs failed as her eyes searched for the bank or something to grab on to. She coughed a few times.

"Help," she yelped.

"Clara!" David shouted, swimming urgently toward her. He rolled her onto her back, supporting her weight as he treaded water. "I have you. Please try and relax your body. It will make it much easier for me to get us to the embankment. I promise, I won't let anything happen to you."

Keep your cool. It's just like you practiced this morning. His hands closed around her now wet and useless cast. *It's so heavy. She did well to keep her head up and out of the water for as long as she did.* A surge of guilt overtook him. *Dr. Evans is going to have to cut this thing off and redo it. I hope I didn't make her injury worse.*

He kicked hard and, carefully as possible, set her down on one of the grassier patches of mud near the pond. Clara coughed a few times and wheezed as he tried to catch his own breath.

"I'm so sorry. Are you all right?" he asked, full of concern.

"Fine." Her teeth clattered. "I'd give anything for a dry towel right now." She wrung out her skirt, splattering a large amount of water onto the ground near her feet.

"I'll make sure you have a stack of clean towels and something hot to drink." He reached into his pocket. His phone was soaking wet and more of a hazard than useful. He rumpled his hair. "I'm going to have to carry you back to the palace or until we find some help. I'll try my best not to jostle your leg."

"What about the wheelchair?"

"It's on the other side of the pond. I don't want to leave you sitting here any longer than necessary. It'll be quicker this way."

She swallowed hard. "Do it."

As if he were carrying the world's most precious cargo, David placed a hand under her legs, and around her back and lifted her to his chest.

"We have to stop doing this, or else you might have to grow a pouch to carry me around like a kangaroo or a koala bear." She laughed, but it sounded forced.

Even when she's freezing, wet, and miserable, she can still manage a joke.

A sudden clap of thunder startled them both. A late summer storm was about to roll through the area.

Bugger off. He picked up his pace.

"If I'm too heavy, you can leave me under a tree and come back for me."

"I'm not leaving you anywhere. I *can* do this. When I was in the army, we did plenty of drills with massively heavy packs. Compared to those, you're as light as a feather."

Behind them, they heard the sound of pounding hooves and a horse neighing. "Whoa there, Clover," a man shouted to his horse.

David knew that voice. His body stiffened, and he stopped jogging. His pulse pounded in his ears. He turned, inclined his head, and panted, "Uncle Reg."

His mother's younger brother smoothly hopped off the sleek chocolate-brown horse and gathered the reins in his hands. He had a stocky build, sandy hair, and hazel eyes. He wore mud-splattered jeans, a camo jacket, and riding boots,

"David, why on earth are you two soaking wet?"

There was no way of avoiding a question from his uncle. "We had a small accident with the canoe."

"That bloody canoe! That thing is knackered. I've *told* you, Edmund, and Alice before. Do *not* take that out onto the water until the carpenters have repaired it," Uncle Reg muttered.

"Yes, sir."

The wind had begun to pick up. His attention turned

settled on Clara's soggy cast. "You, young lady, need to be brought inside now. Have you ever ridden before?"

"Does a pony when I was about eight years old count?" she asked.

Uncle Reg didn't respond.

David fought to maintain a straight face. "At least that's more experience than some of the troopers at the Army's Royal Riding School enter with."

Uncle Reg rolled his eyes. "If David and I give you a hand up, would you be comfortable riding in front of me? This is an English saddle, so there isn't a horn you can hold on to, but I've been riding horses over forty years, and I will ensure you won't fall off."

In his arms, Clara's body trembled. As much as he personally wanted to see to her care, this wasn't about him. It was about doing what was best for Clara.

"Uncle Reg has the best seat in the family. My cousin Alice rode with him when she was two. If a toddler can ride with him, so can you."

Clara took a long moment to study Clover. "Is this a horse that will accept two riders?"

"For short distances, she'll manage." Uncle Reg patted her hind legs.

"Then I'll ride with you."

In a single fluid motion, his uncle was in the saddle again, scooting himself a few inches back. "David, lift her up," he ordered in a commanding tone.

Ignoring the building pain in his shoulders, he adjusted his hold on Clara and handed her to his uncle. A well-trained mount, Clover stood still, tail swishing side to side.

"Hold on to her neck. We'll take this in at an easy trotting pace." Clara gritted her teeth and nodded, her face pale. "David, we'll meet you back inside." His uncle tugged on the reins and made a clicking nose, and squeezed the horse with his legs. "Let's go."

David's arms dropped by his side. He stood and watched, the riders and horse becoming smaller and smaller.

"I'm sorry," he whispered.

Droplets of water hit his face. Lowering his head, he took off to the far side of the pond to retrieve the wheelchair, then set off for the palace. The muscles in his body screamed from overuse. He welcomed the pain as his punishment.

~

"David!" bellowed a strong, authoritative voice. "You have five minutes to change. I expect you in my office in exactly five minutes. Step to it!"

David sat outside of Clara's makeshift room, sick with worry. His hands gripped his hair as he berated himself for his mistake. He was still soaking wet.

"Sir, no disrespect, but I'd rather wait until Dr. Evans is finished with Clara."

"You sitting here soaked through serves no purpose. You'll only make yourself sick. Go change. My study—four-and-a-half minutes." His uncle strode with purpose into the king's apartments.

There was little use trying to argue with the head of the family. David sprinted down the corridor and up one flight of stairs. With skills he learned from his time at Sandhurst, he threw on a T-shirt and trousers and ran a comb through his hair. Glancing at the wall clock, David saw had one minute to present himself to the king.

He sprinted with his last reserves of energy. Outside the

oak door to his uncle's study, he placed his hands on his knees, panting from the all-out effort. He straightened himself out and knocked.

"Enter!"

The private study of King Reginald I was a museum in itself. The furniture had not changed since Victorian times. Photos and mementos on loan from the various branches of the British military adorned the walls.

His diligent staff rotated the displayed items once a month. Photos of his children and other family members covered his large desk. Changed from his dirty riding clothing, he stared into the fire with his hands clasped behind his back.

"You've still got it. Thirty seconds early," the king said as he pivoted to face David. He was a man of few words, and if he hadn't been born into the royal family, Uncle Reg would have been the top-ranking general within the army.

"Reporting as ordered, sir," David exclaimed. When his uncle was in a mood and in "king mode," as they called it, he was addressed as such.

"Sit."

David nervously ran his hand through his hair and took a seat on the couch. His uncle poured a glass of brandy from his private stock and offered it to him. "Drink, then explain from the beginning what happened this afternoon."

David sighed. He wasn't going to be able to do anything until his uncle was satisfied. He accepted the amber liquid and relished how it warmed his insides. He placed the glass on the desk as his uncle took a seat.

"Sir, the young woman you assisted back there is the one I mentioned last week. Her name is Clara Little. I invited her here to watch the Changing of the Guard, chat with Eddie, and give her a tour of the gardens." David paused and considered his wording.

"I had it all planned. I was going to take her out onto the pond for a romantic ride. We'd spend some time chatting, then after enough time had passed, I'd muster up enough courage to tell her that I, er... have started to develop some feelings for her. I'd hoped to ask her out on a formal date sometime next week."

"I see." The king stood and walked out from behind his desk. "And how long have you been interested in her?"

His ears burned. "A week."

Uncle Reg chuckled. "I never would've thought you'd be one to fall for a woman as quickly as Edmund."

"Nor did I. It just... happened."

His uncle remained standing. He brushed his hand over the corner of the closest picture frame. "That's the funny thing about love. It works in mysterious ways. When you find that someone who you truly love, you need to do everything in your power to hold on to her."

David listened intently. His uncle rarely spoke with so much emotion. "When I met Clara, it was almost like she was a magnet, and I was being pulled to her. I just saw her, and I instantly knew she was special. Spending time with her has proven that she's sweet, empathetic, smart, funny, and amazingly talented. I just can't help but wonder if I'm moving along too quickly."

"Trust your instincts and do what you think is right. Your young lady will tell you how fast or slow she wants things to progress. She might surprise you." A thin smile stretched out across the king's face. "Keep me updated on how things unfold. You deserve to be happy."

"I will, Uncle." He stroked his jaw. "Just, uh... one other thing."

"Yes?"

"If Mum starts to meddle, can I count on you to help, er… deflect some of her excitement?"

"Yes. Leave Lottie to me." He poured himself some brandy. "Is there anything else?"

"No, sir."

"You're dismissed."

David gratefully exited the room in all due haste. He speed-walked back to Clara's room to resume waiting to speak to Dr. Evans. How could he get her to forgive him this time? He'd already taken the flower route. He needed to do something bigger and better. Would she appreciate a pair of shoes he'd made? That was one secret she didn't yet know about.

Chapter Twenty-Two

CLARA

"You have a clean bill of health, other than the need to replace your waterlogged cast. Let's try to keep this one dry," Dr. Evans said, winking. "The good news is that your foot appears to be healing nicely."

"That's a relief. Thank you so much. I appreciate you making a house call. I'm sorry to be one of those troublesome patients."

"Nonsense. It's a pleasure taking tea here at the palace when I'm able to. The company of Princess Charlotte and King Reginald is always excellent!"

"How's Jenna doing?"

Dr. Evans's smile widened. "She's doing well. I've never seen her so motivated. She very much enjoyed working with you to learn the Cupid variation. Last night, I caught her trying to learn the Aurora variation from the internet."

It sounds like something I'd do when I was her age.

"The Aurora variation can be tricky. There are so many little nuances that don't always translate well from video."

Clara adjusted her position so she sat taller in the bed. "We can do another one-on-one class together if she'd like."

"Only if you're certain you have time. Jenna knows you are on vacation."

"I do," Clara affirmed. "She's a joy to work with."

"Then in that case, I'll pass the message along. I'm positive she'll say yes." Dr. Evans closed his black leather doctor's bag. "Do you have anything else you'd care to discuss or have me look over?"

"No. Having some time off and just doing some light stretching has taken away most of my aches and pains. My body was more broken down than I think I'd realized or cared to admit."

"I'm glad to hear that. I'm only a call away if you need me." Dr. Evans stood. "Once I open the door, your entourage is going to ask to see you. Are you up for having any visitors or would you prefer to rest?"

Clara's brow furrowed. "That depends on who it is."

While the tumble into the pond wasn't David's fault, she was irritated he'd brushed off her initial concerns about the canoe.

"At last check, Leeds was lingering in the hallway. Princess Charlotte is working out of her office, but asked me to pass on that she'd like to have a few minutes of time to chat with you. The king asked me to see him on my way out. I suspect he'll also ask for an update on how you're faring."

Her head spun. She had half the royal family concerned about her well-being. How was this her life right now?

"I'll wait on David and Eddie until later. However, I'm happy to see Princess Charlotte."

"As you wish, Miss Little." Dr. Evans opened the door and quickly closed it behind him. She could hear David's disappointed voice speaking to the doctor, expressing a desire to see her.

Ten minutes later, the Princess Royal entered the room. "It seems like the men in this family are forever making mistakes. My son should have known better than to trust that rickety old canoe on the pond! I'm just as peeved at him as you must be."

"I am frustrated with him. He didn't listen to any of my concerns. He just brushed them off. I know it's petty of me to not want to see him right now, but I feel like he deserves it."

Although it's also satisfying knowing that he is worried about me. It shows me that he cares. A lot.

"Just so. I'll see to it that David gives you space for the remainder of the day."

"Thank you."

"Do you think you'll be able to manage his company for the ballet tomorrow evening?"

"Yes. There isn't anything that will keep me from it. I just need time to cool down." "Wonderful. This room is yours as long as you'd like. You may even spend the night if you wish."

Clara thanked her again.

"Before I take my leave, I just have one other question to ask you." Princess Charlotte touched her arm. "Shall I collect you for shopping in the morning or the afternoon?"

Her brain couldn't compute what the princess was asking. "Shopping?"

"For your gown for the ballet," she said patiently.

Clara rubbed her eyes. "I didn't realize I needed a gown."

"My dear, you'll be sitting in the Royal Box with my very *single* son. Every eye in the theatre will be on you." Her eyes sparkled with mirth. "I won't send you out in public without making sure you're prepared."

"And if I said that I didn't *need* a dress?"

"I'd counter by gently reminding you that I don't have any daughters of my own. I've been *deprived* of the opportunity to shop for a dress for another female."

Clara was too tired to argue with the Princess Royal. "No matter what I say, you'll find a way of talking me into shopping, won't you?"

"Yes, I will." Princess Charlotte chuckled. "I can be quite persuasive."

"The morning would be ideal."

"Brilliant."

∽

Later that Night

David: I promised Mum I'd leave you be, but I just wanted to check that you made it back to the hotel safely.

Clara snapped a picture of herself snuggled up on the sofa in the living room with her ballerina teddy bear.

Clara: Safe and sound.

David: *Thumbs-up emoji*

Three dots blinked. David was typing.

David: I'm sorry again.

Clara: Apology accepted.

David: Can I still see you tomorrow?

Clara: You'd better believe it. I fully intend to maximize every moment I can with you until I have to go home.

David: *Heart emoji*

Clara stared at her screen. Just what did David mean by

sending her a heart? Was it that he was happy they'd made up? That she wanted to see him tomorrow? Or was it something more?

We almost kissed today. He was so close to me. Those full lips. The sculpted jaw. Those crystal-clear blue eyes. Does he feel the same way I do?

She left the conversation alone for the night. She'd get her answer tomorrow.

∼

Beginning at ten the next morning, Clara and Princess Charlotte were taken to some of the top designer shops in Sloane Square. Dior, Hermès, Chanel, Louis Vuitton—all of the famous Paris design houses had a shop in the area. However, no dresses seemed to suit Clara's build or personality just right.

"Your Highness, could we perhaps take a detour to one of the local London designers? I've always had good luck in small boutiques."

"You wish to wear an unknown British designer?"

"Yes?" she answered carefully.

"Well then, I know just the area. Abigail, my assistant, is always raving about some of the shops off Portobello Road near the market. Let me see if she can recommend someone to us."

Around one that afternoon, Clara and Princess Charlotte entered the Clarissa Lee Atelier. A petite Asian woman and a tall blonde greeting them with bows.

The Asian woman spoke first. "Your Royal Highness, it is an honor to have you in my humble shop. I'm Clarissa, and this is my assistant, Sonya."

Greetings exchanged, Princess Charlotte and Clara

seated themselves on the two light-pink sofas in the center of the room. Between them was a glass coffee table containing an afternoon tea service with a large assortment of sandwiches and confectionaries still warm from the oven.

The Princess Royal poured herself a cup of tea and selected a cucumber sandwich to enjoy. She nonchalantly crossed her legs and drank her tea. "Now then, Clara will be attending the ballet with this evening and requires a suitable gown. My son will be wearing black-tie attire."

The designer's eyes roved Clara's body. "Are you opposed to any particular styles or cuts?" she asked. "Do you have any specific requests you would like us to accommodate?"

Clara hesitated. "If it's not too much trouble, can you give me curves?"

Clarissa smirked. "If there is one task I am suited for, it is dressing a petite body. I can absolutely give you curves." She rubbed her hands together and called to her assistant, "I think we should pull the purple, the aqua, and the pale yellow dresses."

Clara grinned. *This designer is my fashion fairy godmother. I know it. Whatever she puts on me is going to look amazing.*

Sonya cleared her throat. "Let's try on the purple first, please. If you'll follow me, I'll show you to the fitting room. Then we can discuss any alterations with Clarissa."

Clarissa came to a halt. Her face colored. "Please forgive me, Princess Charlotte. I should have consulted you first."

Princess Charlotte, enjoying her tea, blinked slowly and waved her off. "I'm just a fly on the wall. Do whatever you need to do, my dear."

In the dressing room, Clara instantly fell in love with a beautiful floor-length purple one-shoulder gown with an open back. A handful of individually made lace butterflies on the bottom of the skirt made her glow.

This is the most beautiful dress I've ever put on. Wait until David sees me! I don't look like a child in this. I look like a woman!

Chapter Twenty-Three
CLARA

At six thirty that evening, Michael and David arrived in the black Range Rover to escort her to the theatre.

David let out a wolf-whistle. "You look beautiful, Clare-bear." His eyes were wide as he eyed her gown and her smile

"You clean up pretty nicely yourself," Clara joked. "What's with the name?"

"Clare-bear"—he cleared his throat and adjusted his bow tie—"is the name that I've been calling you in my head since the night of the performance. I, er… hope you don't mind."

"Clare-bear," she repeated. "I've never had a nickname before. I like it."

He let out a fake sigh of relief as she slid into the back seat of the car. Sitting next to him, she was fully able to appreciate the way David's form-fitting black tuxedo accentuated his swimmer-like physique. It wasn't lost on her that he even had a purple pocket square, complementing her dress.

"I didn't know you and Mum would be shopping this

morning, or else I would've warned you that she doesn't do anything by halves. When she shops, it's for a complete head-to-toe outfit." He touched the layered ends of Clara's dark brown hair. "I used to look for every possible excuse when I was younger to try and get out of it."

"I felt like a doll. I didn't want to admit it, but I really enjoyed it. Growing up, my mom never liked shopping. She left everything up to me, except when it came to finding a tutu for a competition or a performance." Clara smiled. "Your mother is very kind. She really went to town trying to make sure that everything I picked up was something I liked."

"I'm glad." David stared out the window. "Did my mother happen to speak to you about the media that will be present tonight too?"

"She did." Clara's jaw clenched. "I'm not too happy about it, but I understand that's one of the necessary evils that comes with the territory of you being who you are."

He grimaced. "It makes me feel guilty knowing that I'm about to feed you to a sea of hungry sharks."

"Actually, your mom came up with a pretty amazing cover story." Clara relaxed. "Princess Charlotte said that her office was going to put out a press release this afternoon announcing the expansion of her dance education charity. It's going to start offering scholarships to students in the US and Canada to be able to come and study at the Westminster Ballet's Upper School. My presence here tonight, as a dancer from LABT, signals the kickoff of that partnership. The first dancer to receive a scholarship is from LABT's academy."

"Mum put a lot of thought into this." He stroked his jaw.

"I'm ecstatic she did. That young dancer who's

receiving the scholarship, Chloe, is one of the sweetest, hardest-working kids you'll ever meet. She danced with me in *The Nutcracker* the last two years. I've watched her turn in from a baby ballerina to such a promising junior."

"You glow when you speak about her. You're smiling so bright that I might need a pair of sunnies."

At the Royal Opera House, the car arrived in the underground garage. David walked to the trunk of the car and opened it. "Can you manage with the crutches in that dress, or would you prefer the wheelchair?"

"For this, let's do the wheelchair. I'm afraid that I'll step on the bottom of the dress and tear it." She touched the silky fabric. "We can't have that now, can we?"

"No, absolutely not," David agreed.

"At least by next week, Dr. Evans said I'll be ready for a walking boot. Apparently, I'm a fast healer."

David's security team met them at the elevator and escorted them to the front entrance of the Opera House. Clara drummed her fingers against the armrests of the chair.

"We'll try and get through the photo call as quickly as possible. I'll have George push you and will be right behind you. Know that in my head, I'm holding your hand tightly, but in public, I won't show any affection. It's one of the only ways of protecting you."

Butterflies fluttered in her stomach. "I understand."

George pushed her along at a slow, even pace, pausing every few meters so she could pose for the photographers. One or two members of the media asked her name and snapped her photo. The majority, however, barely acknowledged her presence. For that, Clara was thankful. When she reached the edge of the carpet, George whisked her inside.

"Well done, Miss Little."

Clara held up her hand and George looked at her. "It's for a high five."

"Ah." He tapped her hand softly with his.

"We'll keep working on that."

"Yes, miss."

He wheeled her over to a window, where she watched David preparing to make his walk. He stood with his chin lifted and shoulders pulled back, posture rigid.

"Leeds looks like he's been given the news that he's to march to the Tower," George said with amusement.

"I would've thought he'd be a great actor at faking it for the camera."

"Leeds? Never. He's a horrible actor. Remind me to show you the video proof sometime." George snorted. "Appearing in public is his worst nightmare. He'll never be at ease in front of a camera unless he's the one taking the photo."

They both watched as his appearance caused a frenzy. Cameras galore photographed him from multiple angles. The flashes were so bright, it made the dark night appear to be almost daylight. She understood why celebrities opted for sunglasses. The press screamed his name, baiting him.

David has to go through this every time he's out in public as the Duke of Leeds. I can only imagine how difficult it must have been growing up, as an introvert.

She knew David had had a choice. He could have easily had told his mother he didn't wish to come tonight and put himself on display for the media to go wild over, but he'd agreed to come.

Her insides melted, as if a person had taken hot fudge and poured it atop an ice cream sundae.

He's here for me.

Inside the lobby of the Opera House, Clara relished being a spectator at the ballet, instead of being a performer.

This is so much grander than what we have in LA. Our lobby looks like a movie theater, but this is a proper performance venue.

There was a dedicated coat-check area, a full-service bar and snack area set up with tables and chairs, and even a gift shop. LABT only sold programs and candy to their patrons.

"Would you care for any refreshments, Miss Little, while you wait for Leeds?" George asked.

"Oh, um… a glass of champagne would be lovely."

"Coming right up."

He settled her in a private room and excused himself. Clara took the time to crack over the cover of the bound glossy-red program.

"Yet another thing the Westminster Ballet excels at," she said to herself.

"And what do we excel at?" a man's voice questioned.

Clara jerked in the chair. She rolled backward an inch. "Mr. Williamson."

"Apologies, Miss Little, I didn't mean to startle you." The artistic director of the Westminster Ballet approached her. He wore a navy windowpane-printed suit and wire-rimmed spectacles.

"Your program. I love that it's filled with the ballet's history, interesting facts, has a bio for every dancer in the company."

"Yes, it *is* something I'm rather proud of." He took an empty chair across from her and seated himself. They shook hands. "You look lovely tonight."

Clara's pulse slowed to a normal pace. "Thank you, sir."

"I won't keep you long." He crossed one leg over the other. "I wanted to commend you on your exquisite dancing during the gala. It's been a week and you have me *still* thinking about how you portrayed Aurora."

She chewed on her lip. "Thank you."

He caught her eye. "I wanted to inquire if the Princess Royal has spoken with you."

"She did. Yesterday."

"And may I ask if you've had some time to consider her words?"

Not really. It was a little crazy, but I'd be a fool to close any doors here.

"Sir—Mr. Williamson." She sat taller. "I'm flattered that I'm even in the running of dancers you'd consider hiring."

He appraised her like an owl. "And? Can you envision yourself dancing opposite Anton?"

"Sir, I think any dancer would leap at that chance." She swallowed hard. "I'll tell you what I told the princess. I'm happy to keep my options open, but right now, I have no plans to leave LABT."

The bell rang, signaling the audience to prepare to take their seats.

"I appreciate your honesty." Mr. Williamson nodded. He stood and brushed off his trousers. They shook hands once more. "Enjoy your evening, Miss Little. If you ever change your mind, for you, the door is always open."

He walked toward the door, passing David and George.

"Was that Mr. Williamson?" David glanced over his shoulder.

"Yeah, he just wanted to see if your mother was here to say hello." She crossed her fingers behind her back. "It took you a long time out there."

George passed her a light gold-colored glass fizzing to life with bubbles.

"You don't know the half of it. Just as I thought I was in the clear and was on my way up to you, the opera house director cornered me for a chat."

David pushed her to the elevator and up to the Royal Box just as the house lights were lowered, and the audience hushed. The orchestra picked up their instruments, the conductor entered, and a moment later, the overture began.

∼

After the final note, the audience leapt to their feet in appreciation and applauded loudly. David and Clara watched the first four curtain calls. Afterward, they were escorted down via private elevator to the back of the stage as the audience continued to clap.

The audience relented after eight more bows, and the exhausted performers cheered and congratulated each other after the curtain closed. The LABT never had curtain calls like that. Were the audiences like this every night? Feeding off an electric crowd like this would certainly elevate her dancing to the next level.

Backstage, the dancers let their guards down and went from stage posture and smiles to relaxed and neutral facial expressions. Mr. Williamson introduced everyone to David while Clara remained off to the side and waited patiently for Anton and Evelyne to make their way over to her.

"Clara Little in the flesh!" Anton flashed a tired but warm smile.

"It's nice to put a name to the face. I'm Evelyne. Anton has told me many good things about you." The dark-haired Welsh dancer exchanged greetings with Clara.

"Everything was true," she joked in mock seriousness. "You two were fantastic tonight."

"I should return the compliments," Anton chimed in, mopping his sweaty forehead. "I showed Evelyne a video of you dancing Kitri from a *Don Quixote* performance we found on the internet. She was quite taken with you. How are you doing?"

"I'm on the mend. It's a dancer's fracture of the fourth and fifth metatarsals. I'll be in a walking boot and back en pointebefore you know it. I need to thank you for everything you did on gala night. I don't think I would've been able to make it through the entire performance."

Evelyne popped into the conversation. "Anton here is one of the best partners we could ask for. I do hope we might see more of you in the future. You would fit in well here." Clara squirmed in discomfort and studied the ground at being complimented by such a star dancer.

The three chatted for a few more minutes before both performers rushed off to their dressing rooms to change and remove makeup.

Was the universe trying to send her a signal that the Westminster Ballet should be her home? There was also the David thing to consider. Whatever was going on between them was complicated.

Her gaze traveled to her golden prince, who chatted animatedly with Mr. Williamson. The more time she spent with him, the more she wondered what was going to happen when her fairy tale came to an end. Was there a chance they had a future together?

Chapter Twenty-Four

DAVID

A few days later, the Range Rover stopped in front of number 120 Savile Row in London's Mayfair district. It was a narrow street lined with elegant, stately Georgian and Edwardian storefronts. This was where the best tailors and shoemakers in the UK were located. Mayfair was rich in history.

"I'm sharing something with you that hardly anyone knows about me," David confessed, his face flushing with anticipation. "I'll explain more when we get inside."

Before Clara could ask another question, he exited the car. He was about to open himself up to her. If she didn't think the art of handcrafting shoes was interesting, he was done for.

They entered one of the oldest shops on the street. Its front window displayed a vintage leather men's traveling case, shoes, and a black top hat. He pulled open the door, and a bell chimed. The clerk bounded out of his seat at the excitement of potential customers. When he discovered it was David, his expression changed from hopeful to disappointed.

"Welcome 'round, Leeds," he greeted.

David half-heartedly waved back, keeping his attention on Clara. He watched as her eyes raked the wall-to-wall models of men's dress shoes in various shapes, colors, sizes, and designs.

"There are so many different shoes," she mused.

"The workshop is this way." David led Clara behind the hunter-green curtains near the register, through the storage room. He slowed his pace so she could keep up with him, feeling a mixture of excitement, terror, and nervousness.

Here goes nothing.

In the back of the storage room, a bookshelf built into the wall was opened to reveal a hidden staircase.

"Very *Sherlock*."

"It is, isn't it?" He cocked his head to the side. "I'd never made the connection before."

"Are you some secret agent?"

"Not exactly." He rubbed the back of his neck. "George, we'll ring you when we're ready to leave."

"Right you are, Leeds." George winked. "Have fun."

He left them to their own devices. David assisted Clara down the five steps into the secret work room and settled her on the well-worn cognac-colored sofa. The air smelled of leather, earth, and beeswax.

He remained standing, a hand on his hip. The room was just how he'd left it a few days ago. It was an orchestra of organized clutter. There were wooden workbenches housing handcrafted tools, blocks of wood, and scraps of tracing paper with different elongated shapes. Near the back wall were rows of meticulously arranged leathers in an array of earthy tones. The machinery the shop used for stitching the shoes together was up one level. When it was quiet, he could sometimes hear the sound of it humming to life.

"You've been extremely patient with me, I appreciate it. Now you can ask whatever you want to know."

"So just a wild guess, but you make your own shoes?" Clara said with a hint of playfulness in her voice.

A grin crept across David's face. "I do."

Clara's eyes sparkled with curiosity. "This is so fascinating! I'll be the first to admit I know next to nothing about how shoes are made, but now I have a million questions."

David relaxed, and his smile grew even wider as relief flooded his body. Clara was genuinely interested in his hobby. "Honestly, I'm relieved to hear you say that you find shoe making fascinating and not boring."

"It's anything *but* boring." Clara shifted her position and stretched her legs over the sofa. "Remember, I'm a ballerina who depends on handmade shoes for a living. I've always been curious about how they're created."

David moved to his personal espresso machine and made the two of them cappuccinos. He handed Clara one and pulled out a chair from behind the desk.

"I guess start at the beginning? What's the first thing you do when you're making a pair of shoes?" Clara sipped her cappuccino.

"Everything starts with tracing a foot and figuring out how it works."

"What do you mean?"

David moved closer to her. "It might be easier to show you." An idea was forming in the back of his mind. "Would you mind if I took a look at your feet?"

Clara wrinkled her nose. "My feet are probably the most unattractive things you'll ever see. Dancers have the worst feet in the world."

David chuckled. "I've seen my share of interesting feet."

"Don't say I didn't warn you." She reluctantly shifted so that her casted leg remained on the couch while her good foot was accessible.

David knelt down and carefully removed Clara's left shoe, as if performing a modern-day Cinderella moment. It felt intimate. Slowly and methodically, he examined her foot, appreciating the intricacies of this fascinating part of the human body.

"It's ugly, isn't it?" Clara's gaze drifted toward her own foot. "At least it's not as red and angry as it usually is. Not dancing has given my blisters a chance to heal."

"I don't think they're bad looking at all. You have a high instep," David whispered, his eyes tracing the graceful arc of her arch. "There is a lot of muscle where your ankle and foot come together. It's swollen. I can tell it's been compensating for your injury." His hand brushed the tender skin of the bunion near her big toe. "Your toe shoes don't fit your foot shape properly. They're too narrow."

"You can tell all that from just from a thirty-second evaluation?"

"It's elementary, my dear Clara. It's not rocket science, it's deduction with a dash of charisma."

She sniggered.

I have one more trick up my sleeve too.

David retrieved Clara's discarded shoe and turned it over to reveal the tread. "Using my mad detective skills, I can see that contrary to most people, you walk with your feet turned out. You walk toe to heel more than you do heel to toe."

"And what does that leave you to conclude?" she challenged.

"That right in front of me, I have a ballerina."

Clara's eyes met his. The tension was building between them. His suit was suddenly uncomfortable and constricting. He didn't know how much longer he'd be able to maintain his composure around her. He jumped to his feet and walked over to his desk, grabbing the first thing he could.

He started to ramble the first thoughts that popped into his mind, "Er, once we have the pattern, we can make a last, which is like a mannequin's foot. Lasts ensure that a shoe is crafted to just the right shape and specifications for the wearer. If everything goes according to plan, a bespoke shoe takes about six to eight months to craft. But if I'm making something for myself, I can get it done in about three months."

"David?"

He froze in his tracks. He hadn't realized he'd walked several laps around the sofa.

Clara covered her mouth with her hand, holding in laughter. "Do you have any shoes that you've made down here?"

"Er…" He bumped into a rolling chair, sending several papers onto the ground. He ignored them and tossed the last onto the work bench with a thud, reaching for his latest project. "Here."

Her lips are so rosy, pink. Just like the sparkly tutu she danced in. He pictured himself taking her in his arms and kissing them.

"These are unbelievable. I can't believe you *made* these." She carefully examined the stitching.

He dug his fingers into the palm of his hand, then realized Clara had said something. "Er, can you repeat that?"

"I was just wondering if you've ever considered making shoes for others?"

"I have some plans in the works to launch an affordable collection of dress shoes under the Leeds name sometime in the next year. I'm hoping the income will fund the Waleeds Trust."

Clara interrupted him. "Waleeds Trust?"

Focus.

He casually leaned against the arm of the sofa. "It's the name for the charitable foundation Eddie and I are co-founding. The names is a play on our titles—Wales and Leeds." He hesitated. "We'll be making the announcement next month. Our first order of business is going to be offering art and music classes for children in hospital. When I was in America, I secured the last big donor we needed to make the program happen."

"David." Clara gazed at him, her eyes filled with admiration. "That's amazing! I can see just how passionate you are about this."

"Eddie will be the public face of the Waleeds Trust. We discussed it at length over the weekend. He's ready to shine a spotlight on the issues that matter and throw himself wholeheartedly into the cause."

She raised an eyebrow. "And what about you? I bet you've done all the legwork. Don't you want some recognition?"

David shook his head. "No. I don't need it. The most important thing to me is that the kids know I'm involved, and that's satisfaction enough."

"You're an amazing man, David." Clara reached out toward him, her fingers gently gripping his arms.

His pulse increased, and his throat grew dry. "Clara, I don't know if this is such a good idea."

"I disagree, Detective." Her hazel eyes were wide. "Just when I start to talk myself out of the fact that I'm falling for you, you have to go and tell me something like this." Clara's eyelids fluttered. "Stop talking and kiss me already."

David didn't need to be told twice. He lowered himself onto the couch next to her, drawn by an irresistible force that had been building for far too long. His fingers traced the curve of her lips, gently sweeping a lock of hair behind her ears. "You are so beautiful, Clare-bear," he whispered.

Their lips brushed against each other, tentative at first, then with a growing intensity that mirrored the emotions they'd both long held in check. It was a sweet and tender collision, like a hydrangea flower swaying to and fro in a warm spring breeze. They wrapped their arms around each other, drawing themselves closer still. Their mouths moved in harmony, performing their own delicate dance. Time seemed to stand still as they savored the moment.

Clara eventually pulled back, her chest rising and falling with the shared breaths between them.

"I've been waiting to kiss you for so long." David's voice came out rough.

"Don't stop."

With a soft, affectionate smile, he shifted Clara so she was on his lap, careful not to disturb her cast. He showered her with more kisses, each one growing more intense than the last. By the end of their third round of kisses, their lips were swollen, a testament to the passion that had ignited between them.

I'm the luckiest bloke alive.

Chapter Twenty-Five

CLARA

Later that afternoon, the sun dipped low on the horizon, casting a warm golden hue across the cool gray stones of a castle with formidable thick walls and towering turrets.

"David, where are we?" Clara placed a hand on the car window, captivated by the view. She'd seen photos of castles before, but this was beyond what she'd imagined—a scene straight out of a fairy tale.

"It's Windsor Castle," David said, leaning forward and pointed to the nearest tower. "It's the world's largest castle, a blend of Gothic, Norman, and Victorian architecture. It's also where Mum was born."

"It's stunning," Clara murmured, her eyes fixated on the towers that seemed to touch the sky.

"I'm glad you approve. I would've brought us here earlier, but I wanted to wait until it was closed to the public."

As the car pulled to a stop, Clara gasped again. An elegant horse-drawn carriage awaited them, its polished ebony gleaming in the soft light. A pair of white horses stomped their hooves impatiently against the gravel.

"David." Her voice was breathless. "You've already given me a tour of Mayfair and treated me to high tea at Fortnumand Mason. Now you're taking me on a carriage ride?"

"It's the best way to see the grounds with the limited amount of daylight we have left. We'll do a full tour of the interior sometime soon."

Michael opened the back door. David exited first. As Clara scooted to the edge of the seat, prepared to slide out onto her good foot, he said, "Let's make this easier on everyone." He carried her over to the waiting carriage.

Wrapping her arms around his neck and resting her head on his chest, she sighed in contentment. She heard the soft sound of his heart beating through the light fabric of his dress shirt. "What am I going to do when I have to hobble around LA without you?"

"Shhhh. No talk of leaving me yet. Tonight is about us and living in the moment. Let your prince take care of you."

Her heart fluttered. A warm, fuzzy tingling sensation filled her body. After they settled onto the plush velvet seats, David signaled to the coachman, and the carriage moved forward. The rhythmic clip-clop of the horses' hooves on the cobblestones created a soothing rhythm, as if nature itself were serenading them.

Clara's eyes sparkled with wonder as she took in the picturesque surroundings of the castle grounds. "It's almost like we've stepped into a private forest. There are so many trees."

"That's one of the things I love so much about this place. It's an escape from the outside world. After my parents divorced, I'd spend hours playing in the woods, riding, and pretending that I was a knight. Uncle Reg even had a treehouse built for me near Frogmore Cottage."

"Your uncle sounds like a very kind and caring man."

"He is," David affirmed. His voice softened. "He's also been like a father to me. It's one of the reasons why Eddie and I are as close as we are."

As the carriage continued its leisurely journey through the park, David and Clara engaged in a quiet, intimate conversation.

"Clara," he began, his eyes searching hers. "There's something I've been wanting to discuss with you."

She sensed the seriousness in his tone and turned her full attention to him. "You can tell me anything, David. What's on your mind?"

He took a deep breath, his gaze never leaving hers. "I've treasured every moment we've spent together over the last week and a half. I think about you constantly. You're even in my dreams. I can't help but feel a deep connection between us."

The weight of his words settled in. "David, I feel the same way. I know that what we have is still new, but you've become so important to me."

A hint of relief washed over David's face as he continued. "Then you're open to considering exploring our connection further and seeing where the road takes us?"

"Yes." She nodded emphatically.

Their fingers brushed against each other's, a silent affirmation of their feelings. But David's brows furrowed with a touch of concern. "There's one thing I want to be sure that you understand. Being a royal comes with certain expectations. I don't have the luxury of having a private life. Once the world finds out we're together, you will be hounded by the press. I'll do everything in my power to protect you, but there are limits to what I'm capable of."

Clara's response was filled with unwavering resolve. "David, I understand where you're coming from. Yes, it scares me, but I also feel that I'm better prepared than you might think. Being a ballerina, I've trained my entire life to have thick skin. Every single thing I do in the studio and on stage is scrutinized." She squeezed his hand. "Taking a chance on a relationship with you is worth any challenges that may come our way as long as you can promise that we'll face them together."

"I'm adding courageous to the list of qualities I admire about you."

Their foreheads touched, their noses nuzzled, and against the soft backdrop of the setting sun, they kissed. Their connection had deepened, and their newfound understanding was blossoming into something deeper.

I just hope that we'll have some time together before we're tested.

∽

Later that Night

Had her foot been healed, Clara might have danced around her room to music from the Spice Girls. She relived the highlights of the day in her mind. Savile Row, kissing David, the carriage ride, and more kissing. Her heart felt so full.

She lay in the giant four-poster bed and called Amanda.

"C! About time! I was wondering if you'd forgotten you had a bestie," Amanda joked over the phone.

"Can you video chat? Or are you busy?" Clara scratched her head. "Wait, where are you right now?"

"Yes, no, and the Pac Skyways business lounge at LAX."

"Business lounge? I didn't know employees were allowed in there."

Amanda laughed. "Flight attendants aren't, but pilots are. My dad is traveling through LAX, so I asked him to sneak me in. You know me. Why pay airport prices for food when I can just use Dad's connections?"

"Is your dad still there? I'd love to say hi to him."

"No, he's already on his way home to Seattle."

Clara hit the green button on her screen. A moment later, Amanda's face appeared. Her best friend had green eyes, freckles, and a lion's mane of red hair.

Amanda would make the perfect Princess Merida if she ever wanted to work at a Disney park.

"Oh… somebody is beaming like they've just won a lifetime supply of pointe shoes! Spill! Is it the pri—" Amanda glanced nervously around her and scooted into a private corner "David?"

Clara sighed. "Yes." She took a moment, searching for the right words to express her feelings. "We've spent practically every day together since I've been here. I have no idea how he's managed to still get his work done." She brought Amanda up to speed on everything that had happened.

Amanda held the camera close to her face. "I never thought I'd see the day you would rather spend time with a man than be in the studio. The last time you were injured, you spent sooooooooo much time doing yoga, Pilates, and forcing yourself to watch your company rehearse because you were afraid you'd miss out."

"I know. I never thought I'd say this, but ballet has taken a back seat to David."

Amanda fist pumped. "Yassssssssss! My bestie is finally growing up. *When* I meet your man, I'm so teaching him our secret handshake."

Clara took a deep breath, her heart racing. "A, I'm worried though. It's all moving so fast. I've never felt this way before about anyone. How do I know if what we have is real?"

"C, love doesn't always follow a timeline." Amanda's voice held a reassuring note. "It can happen quickly, and it can be intense. Trust your feelings and your instincts. They're always right. What does your heart tell you?"

Clara's voice trembled. "My heart tells me David is one of those people that I was supposed to meet. That our meeting wasn't by chance."

"And?"

She slid lower into the bed. "And that I am worrying about the hypotheticals. I need just go with the flow and let things happen."

"You said it." Amanda readjusted her phone and rested her arms on the table. "It's okay to have doubts, C. Love is a leap of faith, and it's natural to feel scared sometimes. What matters is how you and David communicate and support each other. If it's meant to be, you'll find a way."

Clara felt comforted by her words. "Thanks, A. I needed to talk this out with you. You're my person. You know me better than I know me."

"Just remember to breathe and take it one step at a time. You don't have to have all the answers right now. Just follow your heart. I believe in you, and I believe in love." Amanda's head disappeared out of the frame for a moment. "Oh, they're bringing out fresh egg rolls and chow mein!"

"Please tell me you're not going to fill up a Tupperware with Chinese food for the plane," Clara groaned.

"Okay, I won't."

"Amanda... I can't believe you."

"What? Lounge food is ten times better than what I'm gonna be eating in economy. I deserve something yummy. Did I mention I'm sitting in the last row of the plane next to the lavatories?" Amanda shuddered. "It's going to be a *long* eleven hours."

"Fine, I guess you deserve it." Clara laughed. "Have a safe flight and I'll talk to you again tomorrow."

"Bye, lady."

Clara disconnected the call. Only after did she realize she'd forgotten to ask Amanda where she was flying to this time.

I bet it's somewhere like Iceland or Norway. She was talking about seeing the Northern Lights last month. I wonder if David has seen them?

As her mind drifted to the thoughts of snuggling under David's arms, sipping on a hot chocolate while watching the Aurora Borealis, she fell into a deep sleep.

Chapter Twenty-Six

DAST: DAVID

Two days later, David opened and closed his mouth as he watched Clara slather a thick layer of gooey Canadian maple syrup over a waffle already topped with strawberries, bananas, pecans, chocolate chips, and clotted cream.

"You don't have any ice cream, do you?" she asked.

"For what?"

"My waffles. What else?" She shot him a quizzical look.

"No." He recoiled. "And even if I did, I wouldn't tell you. Don't you think you have enough toppings on your waffles?"

"I have a sweet tooth."

He stared down at his own waffles. There were a few strawberries to the side, with a spoonful of clotted cream.

"Do you want any syrup?" Clara offered him the container.

"No." He slid the plate closer to him. "It's too sweet. The clotted cream is all I need."

"You're not going to put the cream on top of your waffles?" she challenged.

"I will once I cut it."

Clara chuckled. "So you're one of *those* people."

He arched an eyebrow. "One of what?"

"The type of person who doesn't like to mix what's on their plate." Clara started to cut her waffle into tiny pieces.

"I mix my food together."

She pointed her fork in his direction. "Then what's your excuse on the waffles?"

"I don't like them soggy."

"Clotted cream won't make your waffles soggy." Clara rolled her eyes. "Syrup, maybe. Ice cream, definitely. But not clotted cream—it's super light and airy."

He smiled. "So it is."

It was conversations like this that made him appreciate Clara. To her, he was David. Not a duke. Not a prince. Just David. She appreciated him for who he was. Not the title that came with it.

"You have some dark rings under your eyes. What's on your mind?" she asked.

"Oh, this and that. Nothing for you to worry about." He reached for his coffee and took a long sip.

Too many thoughts weighed on his mind. Clara said she could handle the nasty press that would inevitably pop up sooner rather than later. While she was in the UK, he could protect her, but what would happen once she returned to America? What about her security? Would she be open to having him hire someone to watch her? Should he arrange to return with her?

Theoretically, I can justify a visit to Southern California to take some of the meetings I postponed because of Eddie.

"You saying that is only going to make me more concerned." Clara stood and hobbled over to David.

Standing on one foot, she started to massage his shoulders. His eyes closed.

"Mmm, that feels so good, Clare-bear."

"You have so many knots back here." She dug her thumbs into the tough muscles between his shoulders and his neck. She knew just the right spots to hit. In her hands, his body was putty. He allowed himself to relax, listening to the sound of her talking. "What are you thinking about?"

"Hmm… oh, Eddie getting ready to leave for the army. The charity launch. A lunch I agreed to attend with Mum. You."

"That *is* a lot. Do you not have some type of secretary or assistant who can help you out?"

"I do." He opened his eyes and placed a hand on Clara's. "But there are some things that I prefer to take care of myself."

Like your safety.

"I've been wondering…" she said.

"About?"

Clara sighed. "Have I been too much of a distraction for you? Are you behind on your work because of me?"

He breathed sharply and signaled for her to sit on his lap. "I don't *ever* want you to say that you're a distraction. How I chose to spend my time is *my choice*. I'm an adult, I know what I'm doing." He took a hold of her hand and drew circles on it. "While you're here, you are my number one priority. I've always made time for everybody else. Just this once, I'm being selfish and doing something for myself."

They leaned in toward one another and kissed. Her lips were soft and tender and tasted of sweet syrup.

When they broke apart, he said, "Your waffles are going to be mushy."

They both stared at her plate and shared a laugh.

∼

A short while later, David's mobile chimed. He stared at it and grinned.

Amanda: Landed.

David: Brilliant. You are right on schedule.

Amanda: You're earning major brownie points from me for this.

David: All part of the plan to win my girl's heart.

Amanda: Have you told her yet? I'm dying to text her.

David: In a minute. She's still eating.

Amanda: I guess we should let her finish first. Text me the second she knows.

David: Yes, ma'am.

Amanda is certainly persistent.

"You're grinning. Good news?"

David glanced up and set his mobile face down on the table. "Very."

I hope she's not upset with me after all this.

He cleared his throat. "By my count, you have about three days left before you're due to fly back to America."

"Uh-huh." Clara's face fell.

"You know, by train, Paris is only about two hours away from here. It seems like a huge shame to be so close and not take advantage of seeing it, especially since you've never been. How would you like to spend the remainder of your visit there?"

She was suddenly on high alert. "Paris? As in Paris, France? As in the City of Lights?"

"Yes. Or as you'd say in French, oui."

"I'd say, when can we leave?"

David enjoyed seeing Clara every time she experienced the joy of something new. The enthusiasm was contagious.

"There's only one caveat. As much as I would love to go with you, unfortunately, I have a few matters to settle here," David lamented.

"Oh." Clara processed the information. "I understand."

Oh no. She doesn't think I'm doing this to send her away early, does she?

"I had one job, and I've mucked this up," David grumbled at himself. "Clare-bear, I should've mentioned that you won't be going alone."

"I won't?"

"No." He shook his head. "I've arranged for you to spend the time with your friend, Miss Collins."

David was cut off by Clara's gleeful squeal. She lunged at him from the chair next to his. Her arms wrapped around him. Caught off guard, he started to fall sideways with her in his hold, but managed to steady them just in time.

"Thank you. Thank you. Thank you. Thank you."

Who would've thought she'd be so happy? Here was a woman who gave him a sense of purpose. A woman who he knew he never wanted to let go of. She was the piece of the puzzle that had been missing from his life.

I think I love you, Clare-bear. No. I don't think... I know.

~

David: You can text her now.
　Amanda: *Grinning emoji*
David: Just a moment. I wanted to double check while

I still have you. Did you receive all the hotel and ticket information from my office?

Amanda: Yup.

David: And it looked satisfactory?

Amanda: *Nodding emoji*

David: Brilliant. Remember, if there is anything else you two need, just ask.

Amanda: *Nodding emoji*

David clicked his mobile screen off and left the kitchen to give Amanda and Clara some privacy. Now all he needed to do was confirm with the security team he'd hired to keep up with the two women.

Should I mention it to them? No. They're probably both better off not knowing. If all goes according to plan, they won't even know the detail is there. If Clara decides this is the life she wants to have, it's better that she thinks she still has some sense of freedom.

Chapter Twenty-Seven
CLARA

Leaving London was difficult. Two and a half of the most magical weeks of Clara's life had been there. Knowing it wasn't a permanent goodbye was the only way she could get herself to depart the St. George. This would mark the greatest physical distance Clara would be from David since they had met.

They had exchanged private goodbyes the night before as she'd left his flat. Despite the excitement she should have felt toward seeing Paris for the first time, as she gazed back at David through the car window and waved until he disappeared from view, an unexpected void seemed to open within her. In that moment, a part of herself she hadn't even known existed suddenly vanished.

I need to test what we have. I need to test myself.

St. Pancras Station was packed with business travelers and tourists walking every which way. There was a constant buzz of conversations. Near the passenger drop-off area, a chaotic scene unfolded as cars, buses, and vans jostled for precious curb space.

Clara reluctantly got out of the Range Rover and had

Michael assist her with her luggage. "Michael, you have been such an amazing person to work with. Thank you for everything."

"Miss Little, you've been a breath of fresh air. I hope to see you in the very near future, if I do say so myself." Michael tipped his cap to her until he observed Clara make it through security and into the passport control area.

Two bored-looking French police officers waved her through without giving her a second glance. The waiting area of the Eurostar was packed, with few seats open. Shrugging, she sat on her suitcase, glad she didn't need to wait overly long.

She sent a text to Amanda.

Clara: Checked in and waiting for my train to depart.

Amanda: *Dancing emoji* Counting down the minutes 'til I'm reunited with my bestie. When you get to the station, there should be a car waiting for you. Your man thinks of everything. The hotel address is in the email I forwarded to you just in case.

Clara: Thanks! Can't wait! See you soon!

She texted David next to let him know her status.

David: I hope you enjoy your time in Paris. Promise me you'll check in with me once a day and stay close to Amanda.

Clara: *Heart emoji* Thanks. I miss you already. I promise I will.

∼

Two beautiful black cats with yellow and green eyes were lying stretched out, sunbathing in the middle of the red and gold carpet as Clara arrived in the lobby of the Hotel Noir

Chat. Hearing her approach, one of them poked its head up, appraising her with interest.

"Bonjour," she said.

As soon as the cat realized Clara didn't have any food, it blinked slowly and put its head back down on the ground, resuming its nap.

"I knew you would love the resident felines that lived here as soon as I saw the picture of them on the hotel website," Amanda said.

Clara pivoted around and hugged her best friend.

"How was the ride over?"

"It was smooth sailing. I don't know how David did it, but a private driver met me on the platform. Considering how much traffic there was, we seemed to zip right over from the Gare du Nord station." She laughed.

"That cast is larger than I thought."

"It is, but nothing is going to stop me from hobbling around Paris with it." Clara shifted her weight on her crutches. "I've gotten better at using these bad boys. I just might have to take more breaks than we'd like."

Amanda rubbed her hands together. "Your man sent ahead a knee scooter and a wheelchair if you decide to ditch the crutches."

"He did?" Clara's heart swelled, knowing that David had poured so much thought and care into this trip.

"Yup." Amanda nodded. "You, my dear C, have hit the jackpot. After working with David on planning your trip, I'm gonna be spoiled for life. No man is ever going to measure up to him."

"I know," she said softly.

"We're in room seven, but before we head up, you need to register with the concierge. She just needs your passport info, then I have big plans for you."

DANCING WITH A ROYAL

Clara gave Amanda her luggage as she checked in. The hotel might not be as luxurious as her London property, but it had a lot of charm and character. The Hotel Noir Chat was tucked away across the street from the Louvre, in a quiet back alley. Once a tavern, it had been converted into a three-star bed-and-breakfast style hotel in the early 1900s.

On the elevator ride to the third floor, Amanda had a difficult time remaining still. She gesticulated wildly as she spoke. "Once you've had a snack and gotten changed, we'll head out. I made sure today's itinerary is light on the walking." The doors opened and they continued down the hallway. "We'll spend the rest of the morning shopping, then this afternoon we'll go and see the Eiffel Tower."

Clara groaned. She loved shopping, but Amanda took it to a whole new level. It was a trait she'd inherited from her mom. Amanda had an eye and a taste for the finer things in life.

There are many high-end fashion designers here in Paris. I hope A doesn't intend to visit all of them.

"Did Mama Collins send you a list of things to check out while we're here?"

"I didn't tell her where I was going, or else shopping would take all day," Amanda said, inserting the key into the door. "We're only going to hit up three stores: Chanel, Louis Vuitton, and Cartier. The Chanel boutique on Rue Cambon is something I want you to see; it's the original store. Coco Chanel used to live above the atelier and have her studio there."

"What about my Musee D'Orsay and the Louvre?"

"That's tomorrow, and after is a day trip to Versailles, also for you."

"Works for me."

Entering the room, Clara gasped. She walked straight to

the balcony, where a breathtaking panorama unfurled before her. The room boasted an awe-inspiring view, overlooking the Seine River and the majestic facade of the Louvre. Clara felt as though she had stepped into a postcard.

"It's every bit as beautiful as I imagined it would be." She leaned against the railing. "Was it David's idea for me to see Paris? Or yours?"

"Mine." Amanda joined her, soaking in the view. "He called me two days ago, asking if there was any way he could convince me to come out and join you for the end of your trip. I told him as long as he paid for one of our dinners, I'd be on the first plane out to London. I was already off the rest of the week."

"Uh-huh. And how did Paris come up?"

"He gave me an overview of the places you've been and things you've done." She shrugged. "To me, it seemed like you'd ticked off most of the boxes of things first-time visitors to London should do, so I suggested that we come and see Paris."

"I feel guilty using your time off to visit a place you've been to a million times." Clara rubbed her forearms. "Where had you originally planned to go?"

"Singapore or Auckland, but that doesn't matter." Amanda brushed her off. "I can get to those cities any old time. I'd much rather spend my vacation with you, especially since this is your first time! I want it to be memorable."

I'm so lucky to have such amazing friends.

"Besides. In the past, every time I've tried to get you to travel, some type of dance emergency seemed to come up. I knew this time, at least, there wouldn't be any excuses for you to skip out."

That's true. I always pushed off traveling to step up and fill in for somebody who's ill or injured. This time, it's my turn.

～

Clara and Amanda glided into the six-story flagship Cartier boutique on the Rue de la Paix. The grandeur of the store was matched only by the sparkle of the treasures within. Diamonds and gems of every hue beckoned to them from behind glass displays, and the scent of luxury enveloped them.

"There are so many pieces of eye candy that I don't even know where to start looking," Amanda gushed.

"I agree with you one hundred percent." A woman in a black uniform chuckled and gestured to the case. "Is there anything you'd like to see up close or try on, perhaps?"

"No." Clara shook her head. "We're just looking."

"Clara. Live a little." Amanda elbowed her. "It doesn't hurt to try on fine jewelry."

"You know we can't afford anything in here." Her cheeks burned.

The sales associate laughed again. "Mademoiselle, I'll let you in on a little secret. On my salary, I can't afford half the items we sell either, but that doesn't stop me from trying a few pieces on."

"I just don't want us to waste your time." Clara stared at the floor. "Time is money, and I'd hate for you to lose out on a sale and the commission that comes with it because you're helping us."

"Mademoiselle, you're kind, but I assure you, it's fine. If you find something you like and decide to purchase it in the future, just remember to come to Cartier. Is it a deal?"

"Oui," Amanda answered on her behalf.

"Now, which case would you like to start with?" The saleswoman removed a ring of keys from her pocket.

Clara's eyes were drawn to an exquisite platinum ring set with diamonds and amethysts. Its deep purple hue was reminiscent of the dress she'd worn the night she went to the ballet with David.

"That one." She pointed to it.

The Cartier sales associate carefully placed the ring on a tray. With clammy hands, she picked it up and slid it onto her right ring finger.

"Size seven. A perfect fit," the woman said.

Clara's heart skipped a beat. Staring at the stone, she pictured David's face, his form-fitting tuxedo, and the kiss they'd shared in his shoe-making workshop. She glanced at herself in the mirror, the amethyst sparkling like a hidden star.

Amanda observed Clara with a knowing smile. She snapped a few photos of her and the ring on her phone. "You're glowing."

Clara nodded, her eyes still fixed on the amethyst. "It's just so pretty. It reminds me of my first real date with David. The dress I wore was this color."

"I think we should look for a pair of earrings to match it. And can I try on that emerald?" Amanda asked.

"Oui."

As they prepared to leave the store an hour later, the Cartier sales associate approached Clara with a small package in hand. "Mademoiselle," she said with a polite smile, "I was just told that this is for you."

Clara, puzzled but intrigued, accepted the signature red shopping bag.

"What is it, C?"

Inside, she discovered a square box wrapped in thick red paper sealed with wax. She held it up for Amanda to inspect. Her friend squealed. "Open it!"

"Shouldn't I wait until later?"

"No! Open it right now!"

The sales associate smiled like a Cheshire cat. Unwrapping the paper and opening the box, Clara discovered a dainty yellow-gold bear-shaped pendant. Its two diamond eyes twinkled, and where its heart would be was an etching of the letter C.

"David," she whispered. A stray tear fell down her cheek. "His nickname for me is Clare-bear."

As Clara held the pendant close to her heart, a profound realization washed over her. In that moment, she knew without a doubt that she was deeply and irrevocably in love with David—her heart belonged to him.

Chapter Twenty-Eight
CLARA

Clara didn't know what to expect as they explored the Trocadéro area. It was an electric feeling, seeing the Eiffel Tower rise over the city in the distance. It seemed surreal to experience such an icon in person.

Amanda squealed in delight and hugged her tightly. "I can't believe he had a custom pendant made for you! Have you tried calling him yet?"

Clara checked her phone again. Her home screen still showed no alerts. "The second we left the shop, but he's not answering. He might be in a meeting." She tucked her phone into her purse and sat on the leg of her new knee scooter.

After taking a dozen photos of one another, they made their way over to the landmark's entrance. Their timed-entry tickets allowed them to explore the belly of the Eiffel Tower thirty minutes before they would be able to take an elevator to the top. They entered the security queue, joining the sea of tourists chatting in a lively manner in multiple languages.

"Pardon, madam." A man in a white T-shirt and jeans approached them with a woman and two kids. "Can you take our photo?" He held out his phone.

"Us too!" Another couple walked up behind the family and headed straight for Amanda.

I can't really say no. That would be rude.

"What do you want in the background?" She moved her handbag behind her.

"Here is fine."

Clara tapped the phone's screen, so it was in focus. "On three. One, two, and three," She clicked the white button.

The kids ran up to Clara as she passed the camera back to the man.

"Is this a toy?"

"Can I try?"

Their parents clapped their hands together. The kids ran back to them.

"Thank you!" the man said, and hastily jumped out of the line. The couple that Amanda had helped also walked away quickly.

"That… interesting." She glanced to Amanda. "The kids thought—"

"C, your purse! It's open!" Amanda exclaimed.

Clara's pulse increased. Her hands scrambled for her purse. "I thought I closed it." Glancing inside, she gasped. "My phone! My wallet! They're gone!"

Both women looked in the distance, spotting the four adults and two children interacting with another family. Clara clenched her teeth together. Everything of value she owned had been in the two items they'd taken.

Pushing off with her good foot before Amanda could stop her, Clara took off on her scooter. "Hey!" she shouted, attracting attention. "Somebody, stop them!" She pointed in front of her. "They're pickpockets!"

The group of thieves froze when they heard Clara's voice. She watched the color drain from their faces. Dozens of eyes turned to stare. They took off running.

"Arretez! Stop!" she called out again in both French and English. She was gaining on them until the wheels of her knee scooter hit the grass, abruptly getting stuck. She gripped the handles tightly, fighting to stay upright. She pounded her fist against her thigh. "Darn it!"

"Clara!" Amanda cried. "Let them go. It's not worth it." Her friend rushed over, panting. "Are you all right?"

"Fine." Anger surged through her body. How could she be so foolish to let her guard down? All she'd wanted to do was be nice and help a family out. But instead, they'd taken advantage of her! She groaned. "All my photos from the trip. My passport. My credit cards. It's all gone."

"It'll be okay," Amanda said comfortingly, touching the small of Clara's back. "I know it sucks now, but we'll figure this out. I've been pickpocketed twice. Once in Spain and once in Rome. The first thing we need to do is find a police officer and file a report. They we'll call your credit card companies and put a freeze on your cards."

Her head was beginning to ache. "David's phone number was in there too. I didn't have it saved in any other place."

"I have it in my phone. I'll give it to you later." Amanda tapped her belt bag. "The couple got my spending cash, but nothing else."

Clara swallowed hard, feeling slightly guilty for not asking about her friend. "Okay."

Suddenly, as if out of thin air, three men dressed as tourists appeared, moving with an air of importance. One of them wore a blue-and-white English Premier League football jersey, the second a green polo shirt, and the third a white button-up shirt.

The man in the white shirt approached them first. "Miss Little. Miss Collins. Are you okay, ladies?" His voice was calm and reassuring.

Clara gripped Amanda's arm. "How do you know our names?" Her voice came out shaky.

The man in the white shirt exchanged a glance with his colleagues before explaining, "We were hired to ensure your safety during your trip to Paris, Miss Little."

Clara's anger began to simmer as realization dawned upon her. "David hired you without telling me?"

"Technically speaking, ma'am, we're not at liberty to discuss the details of the arrangement. You and Miss Collins were never supposed to know we were tracking your movements unless it was absolutely necessary."

"You've been following us the entire time?!" Clara's frustration grew, her voice sharp as she retorted, "I can't believe he didn't trust me to handle my own safety. This is ridiculous!"

Amanda stepped in. "Clara, maybe David just wanted to make sure we had a worry-free trip."

"I'm sure he did, but that's not the point! By hiring a security team without telling us, I can't help feeling like he doesn't trust me. We're big girls, we can take care of ourselves!"

Clara heard the sound of a phone ringing. The man in the football jersey excused himself.

"Miss Little, I apologize that we weren't able to react and get to you any quicker." The man in the white shirt held out his hand. "I'm afraid we were only able to retrieve your mobile phone. Not your wallet."

She took the item and hugged it to her chest. "Thank you."

Some of the tension fled her body. At least she'd still have her photos. She'd never forget to back up her phone again.

The man in the blue jersey cleared his throat. "Miss Little, I have... our boss. He'd like to speak to you."

"Tell him I'm not in the mood to speak to him. I have other things I need to do first." She huffed and caught Amanda's eye. "We need to go file that police report."

"Would you like us to give you a ride to the closest station?" the man in the white shirt asked.

"Yup," Amanda answered. "If you're going to be following us anyway, we might as well make this easier for everybody."

Clara was left with mixed feelings. On the one hand, she felt gratitude that David cared that much about their safety, but on the other, she was annoyed at his lack of trust.

One little conversation is all it would've taken. That's it. He can't be my protector forever. I'm not in London anymore. I'm in the real world, where sometimes bad things happen. If he wants to be a part of my life, he's going to have to learn to accept that.

~

Later that afternoon, back at the hotel, Amanda offered to run and grab dinner from the restaurant in the lobby. Neither felt like venturing out again after the excitement of earlier.

Clara sat on a chair on the outdoor balcony. She held her phone tightly, her knuckles white as she dialed David's number. After a few tense rings, he finally answered.

"David... we need to talk." She tried her best to keep her voice neutral.

"Clare-bear, please tell me you're okay. I've been worried about you and Amanda all day. It's taken everything in me not to jump on a plane over to Paris."

"You don't need me to answer that. After all, I'm sure you're receiving regular updates about me from your security team."

"Clare-bear," David replied cautiously. "I know you're none too thrilled about the team..."

"That is the understatement of the century," Clara snapped, her voice laced with resentment. "How could you not tell me?!"

There was a pause on the other end of the line before David responded. "I didn't want to worry you. Please understand—I did it because I care about you! Paris is a dangerous city. Look at what happened this afternoon!"

"Petty crime can happen anywhere at any time."

"Yes, but it didn't happen to just anyone. It was you."

"David—"

"Look, Clare-bear, I'm trying hard to be understanding. I apologize for not telling you, but I'm not sorry for being concerned about you or for having the team there. I'd do it again in a heartbeat. Once you get used to them when you're back in LA, you'll find that it really isn't so bad to have—"

"What? Security in LA?"

David sighed. "I was waiting for you to be a little more levelheaded before we discussed it."

"No! You've done it again!" Her nostrils flared. "There is no discussion because it's not going to happen."

"Clara..." His voice was cracking.

"Answer me this: Have you already hired the guys?"

"Yes."

"Then this conversation is pointless." Her heart was breaking. "I can't be with a man who doesn't value me as an equal partner, or a man who makes decisions for me. There isn't any room for secrecy in our relationship."

"Clara, I'm sorry."

"I am too. I really thought… well, forget it." A few tears began to leak out of the corners of her eyes.

"So that's it? Just like that? Are you're breaking up with me?"

"I guess I am," she sniffled.

Heavy silence passed between them.

"I know you're angry and that we both need time to cool off. If this is what you want, I'll step aside. You're a very special woman. I respect you and I love you. You've captured my heart, and you're the only woman who it will ever belong to. You have my mobile number. All you have to do is say the word, and I'll be by your side in an instant."

The waterworks began to flow. "Goodbye, David."

"Goodbye."

She disconnected the call. Her body shook. Her phone fell to the ground. If this was the right thing to do, why did it physically hurt so much?

~

Clara's heart was no longer in the mood to enjoy Paris. Going through the motions with Amanda, she tried her best to put up a strong front. The remaining two days passed in a blur. It was time for her to return home and back to her life in Southern California.

"I'm not ready to talk about it," Clara said tiredly at the airport before her flight.

Amanda took a deep breath. "Okay. I'll leave you be, but holding in your emotions is not healthy."

"I know." Clara gripped the arms of her crutches tightly. "I just need time to sort through everything that's happened. When I'm ready, you'll be the first person I call."

"I made sure that the gate agents and cabin crew know to give you the VIP treatment." Amanda wrapped her arms around her bestie and hugged her tightly. "Let me know when you get home. I'll be a couple of hours behind you. I have to do a stopover in Dublin."

"I will."

Clara's eleven-hour flight from Paris to LA gave her time to reflect on how much her life had changed in the three weeks since the gala. She'd danced on the stage of the Westminster Ballet, had met a prince, injured her foot, and as the cherry on top, she'd fallen in love. Her life was beginning to sound like one of those predictable holiday romance movies.

It's all for the best. I'm not the type of girl who'd be duchess material anyway. All I've done my entire life is dance. Without it, I have nothing. We're from two different worlds. How would our relationship really have gone anyway? The long-distance thing would've been difficult to figure out.

Clara made herself a mental checklist. She needed to reestablish her old routine and start getting back into dancing shape. She was a soloist and had an example to set at LABT. She also couldn't risk giving Artum another reason to push back the start of her new contract.

Tomorrow I'll make an appointment with the company doctor and see if this cast is ready to come off. Once I'm in a walking boot, I can start some physical therapy.

Chapter Twenty-Nine

DAVID

"Edmund. Excellent, you're five minutes early," King Reginald said, looking up from his desk and beckoning his eldest child inside.

"Father." Eddie inclined his head.

David smiled at his cousin and patted the chair next to him. Eddie entered the room and took a seat.

"I'm so proud of how much you've turned yourself around these past few weeks. Well done, indeed." The king grinned. "David has briefed me in on the plans and causes the Waleeds Trust intends to patronize during its initial launch. It shows real initiative that you lads have come up with this all on your own. I'm happy to lend the full weight of the crown behind it."

"Thank you, sir. David and I truly hope we can make a difference, even if it's a small one," Eddie said, sitting tall.

You're looking every inch the Prince of Wales these days.

"Edmund, now that you're here, I'd like to hear what your thoughts are about your send-off to Sandhurst." Uncle Reg cleared his throat. "Your mother and I agree that we'll keep the gathering small and limited to family and a few of your close friends. Would you prefer to host it here at Windsor, or at Sandringham?"

David placed a comforting hand on Eddie's knee, lending his cousin his silent support. This was a battle his younger cousin would have to fight on his own.

Eddie slowly pushed his chair back, stood, and straightened his shoulders as he spoke. "Father. I was hoping we could speak about that before you go any further."

Uncle Reginald raised an eyebrow. He glanced first to David, then at his son, and nodded. "Certainly. What's on your mind, son?"

Eddie's Adam's apple bobbed up and down. "Father, I've decided that I don't want to attend Sandhurst."

The king coughed. "Excuse me?"

"Sir, I know that it's rather late notice—"

"Your military service is non-negotiable!" The king stood so fast that his chair topped backward, clattering onto the ground. "You are the future head of state and commander of the armed forces. How do you expect to serve your country if you haven't served or worn the uniform?"

Eddie didn't flinch at all at his father's harsh tone. David was impressed, but could see his cousin needed a moment to compose himself.

"Uncle, if you would hear Eddie out. He wasn't finished speaking when you cut him off."

"Very well." The king picked up his chair and resumed his seat.

"Father, please listen and do *not* interrupt me until I'm finished speaking," Eddie commanded sternly, locking eyes with his father. "I did *not* say that I *didn't* want to serve my country. I just want to do it in my own way." He placed his arms behind his back. "Instead of enrolling in the officers' course at Sandhurst, I want to enlist and work my way up through the ranks. If I become an officer, it'll be a non-commissioned one. The most effective leaders earn the respect of others, and that's *exactly* what I intend to do."

"Enlist?" Uncle Reginald asked, confused. "Non-commissioned officer?" For the first time in recent memory, the king was too stunned for words.

"Yes, sir," Eddie said in a patient tone. "I've done my research, and I believe the best fit for me would be the Household Cavalry Mounted Regiment. You and David were both members of the cavalry, and I'd like to continue the family tradition you two established."

"I see. And which regiment would you choose? The Blues and Royals or the Life Guards?"

David chuckled. *Which regiment indeed. Your dad was a member of the Blues and Royals, but I was a Life Guard. The two regiments may both be under the cavalry umbrella, but there is a lot of pride at stake here.*

"The Life Guards, sir. It's the oldest."

David kept observing, allowing Eddie to guide the conversation. He circled around to where his father sat on the other side of the desk.

"And are you aware it's the most difficult course in the British Army?" The king stroked his chin.

"Yes, sir. I've spoken to several different officers at the Ministry of Defense. I understand exactly what the course entails," Eddie pointed out matter-of-factly.

"And this is your final decision? Nothing I say may sway you? You understand arrangements have been made for months at Sandhurst for your own safety and security."

"Father, I will not be deterred, and yes, I understand the hardship I'm placing on you and everyone involved in the logistics, but this is *my* future. I deserve to have a say in the decision, as you have taught me."

David held his breath. It struck him that the situation Eddie was in shared many similarities with Clara's. When she'd voiced her frustrations with him about her security, it had been over his making a decision for her. He was beginning to have a better grasp on where she was coming from.

What is she up to now? We haven't spoken in over two weeks. I miss her so much.

"All right."

"That's a yes?" Eddie asked gleefully.

"Yes, son, that is a yes. When all is said and done, you'll be the first member of the royal family to ever enlist. I'll see to it that everything is taken care of. I'm quite proud of you, you know. I may be tough, but it's my way of showing how highly I think of the man you have become."

"Thank you, Dad." Eddie hugged his father.

David took everything in, smiling. "Well done, Eddie." He clapped him on the back when his cousin released his uncle.

Opening his liquor cabinet, the king pulled out one of his favorite bottles of sparkling wine and poured each one of them a celebratory drink. They toasted one another, and David shared a few memories of his time in the cavalry with Eddie.

"David and I have a few more items to discuss. But before you leave, I need an answer from you. Where shall we host your party?"

Eddie placed his glass down and said in a cheeky tone, "How about my apartment at Kensington Palace? I can even make the arrangements myself."

"Kensington Palace is fine, but your mother is adamant that she should be the person in charge of planning the affair. If you'd like to take the responsibility from her, it's up to you to try and sway her."

Eddie deflated. "On second thought, forget I ever asked. Mum can be in charge of the arrangements."

"Smart lad. Never anger the women in your life. That's a lesson I have learned the hard way over time. You are dismissed. Please, shut the door behind you."

David fidgeted. Eddie gave a thumbs-up to his cousin on the way out and happily left.

Uncle Reg smirked at the closed door. "Who would have thought my son would ask me to enlist in the army?" He shook his head.

"One last topic of conversation this afternoon," the king continued, turning to David. "How is your situation with Miss Little coming along?"

"It's not."

"And have you made *any* attempts to apologize to her?"

David rubbed his temples, the emotional exhaustion of the last fortnight sinking in. "No, Uncle. I haven't."

"Well, that's your problem." The king placed a hand on his shoulder. "You can't just leave the situation alone. You have to help it along and do everything in your power to try and win her back, even if it's from a distance."

"I don't even know where I'd begin."

Uncle Reg chuckled. "As much as you may not want to hear this, if I were in your shoes, I'd get some advice from the experts—your mum and your aunt."

David cringed. "How did I know it was going to come to that?"

At this point, he would do whatever it took to get his Clare-bear back, even if it meant that he'd have to concoct a crazy scheme with his mother.

Chapter Thirty

CLARA

Clara's stomach performed somersaults. Her eyes traveled down the length of her leg to the worn-out purple cast.

A door opened and closed. "Clara, welcome back. We've missed you at LABT, but I've heard glowing reviews about your performance in London." The ballet company's therapist pulled out a stool from underneath the exam table and sat down. "Dr. Brown is reviewing the most recent set of X-rays and scans you took at the medical clinic yesterday. He'll swing by in a few minutes for a physical exam. In the meantime, let's get this nasty old cast off. Dancers are fast healers, and I'm pretty confident in saying that you'll leave here with a boot."

"I'm *more* than ready to be able to shave my legs again and to take a shower," Clara joked.

Rifling through a drawer full of tools, the physical therapist brought out a small saw and, in less than a minute, cut her way through the thick fiberglass. The change in pressure was immediate.

"Oh, that's so much better," she exclaimed, lifting her much lighter leg.

"Emily said the same thing when I removed her wrist cast." Using a dampened cloth, the PT took a few moments to clean the leg. "There. All better."

Holding her breath, Clara took her first proper look at her foot. She'd known the muscles would atrophy, but seeing it in person made the reality of her situation sink in. There would be no easy road back to the stage. It would take her weeks, if not months, to build up not just her calf muscles, but all the tiny muscles in the foot too.

"Clara!" Dr. Brown walked over to the exam table and shook hands with her. "How are you today?"

"Hi, Dr. Brown. I've been better."

"I know that look." He walked over to the sink, washed his hands, and dried them with a towel. "I know it's unnerving to see your leg so weak, but trust me, it's perfectly normal." He ran his hand along the joint line and carefully palpated her toes. "The bones feel good. Ligaments are tight, but normal. So far, so good. Any persistent pain?"

Clara leaned back on her elbows. "No pain in my foot. I did have some pain in my lower back, but that went away the second week I had the cast. I think my body was just getting used to the unusual way I had to move with it."

"If it returns, let me know."

The doctor walked over to the computer opposite the exam table and pulled up her scans. "This X-ray was taken right after you were injured." He clicked and changed images. "And this one is from yesterday. Comparing the two scans, the hairline looks to have completely healed."

Clara fist pumped. "Does that mean I can started in on PT?"

"Yes, Clara. It does." The doctor grinned. "I'm clearing you to go ahead and start with some slow, basic weight-bearing exercises. It's going to take time to regain strength. Remember that you have to walk before you can dance. I'm going to put you in a walking boot for two weeks. It can be removed when you're doing PT and at night, but otherwise you should keep it on."

"Got it. What about the crutches? Can I ditch them?"

"Soon. You'll need them for a few days. I'd like you to start with partial weight-bearing with the boot and slowly transition back to normal walking. We don't want to overload your body and cause a setback."

"Understood."

"Do you have any other questions for me?"

"No."

"Okay, then I'll leave you two ladies to get to work. Feel free to email or call me if you need anything."

He left the room.

"I'll get you fitted for a boot in a few minutes," the therapist said. "But before that, I'm going to show you a few mobility exercises you can do at home. I'll start you off with coming in to see me three times a week. We'll work on getting your foot back to normal, but also on building up the supporting muscles too. Now is when the real work begins."

As Clara tested her leg for the first time in four weeks, she was happy that she was able to stand unassisted. It was weak from lack of use, but held. She felt like a child learning to walk again.

Each step is a milestone. I'll be back by the winter season. I know I will.

The following Wednesday morning, the artistic director's overly friendly secretary waved her in. "Good morning, Clara. I just heard the news. Congratulations! The phone has been ringing nonstop! Artum will see you now."

Puzzled, she managed to say, "Um… thanks."

"This is the Los Angeles Ballet Theatre, how may I direct your call this morning?" The secretary had already turned her attention back to her phone.

Pulling the door open, Clara entered Artum's office. Posters of the company's past productions for *Swan Lake*, *Coppelia*, *The Sleeping Beauty*, and *The Nutcracker* adorned the wall. He signaled for her to take a seat.

"Yes, we're very fortunate. Uh-huh. Uh-huh. No, the signed pointe shoes would only be sent to you for a donation above ten thousand." Artum held up his hand. "Certainly, we can have them personalized for your daughter. Uh-huh. Uh-huh. Great, well, if you have any other questions, just give my secretary or the donor relations department a call."

Clara folded her hands on her lap. Her leg jittered up and down. Was he going to want an ETA when she could be back? She didn't have an answer for him. It was all wait and see. Worst case, she supposed maybe he'd just push the soloist contract back again a couple months.

In the meantime, maybe I can ask about teaching a class with the LABT school this fall to stay busy. I really liked working with Jenna, and I'd like see if it's something I enjoy doing long-term.

Since she'd been back in LA, Clara had found herself beginning to spend some time wondering exactly what her future held for her. What was going to happen after her body could no longer handle the demands of a professional career? It was a question she'd pushed aside, thinking that she had *years* before she'd ever have to give such thoughts any consideration, but now, everything had changed.

With only PT to fill her days, she had more free time than ever. Her friends made time for her when they could, but they worked full-time jobs. Her dance friends were in rehearsal during the day and performed at night.

Clara read books, went shopping and to the movies, but it did little to help quell her feelings of loneliness and isolation. She'd been so focused on her career that she'd lost sight of the fact that without dance, there was a gaping hole left behind.

I'll call David today. Even if I'm still a little mad at him, I just can't stand it anymore. I need to hear his voice. I need him in my life. I should never have pushed him away. I love him too much to go through life without him.

"Sorry about that." Artum hung up the phone.

"No problem. I have nothing but time at the moment." Clara attempted to sound enthusiastic as she wiped her palms on the side of her yoga pants.

"How long have you been with us, Clara? I've lost count. Is it three seasons?"

"Actually, it's five."

Artum laughed. "I'm pretty sure it hasn't been that long, but however many seasons you've been with us, we've come to appreciate everything you've done at LABT."

It's five seasons, but it wouldn't do well to correct him.

"Well, I have loved being part of LABT. You've given me a lot of opportunities, and I'm so excited that I'll be able to continue to grow as a soloist."

That much was true. She dearly appreciated LABT for being the only company that initially offered her a contract out of the Seattle Ballet Academy.

"When you called me a couple weeks ago, I'll be the first

to admit that I was worried that I might've been wasting a contract on a dancer who was past her prime. You have to admit, twenty-seven is pretty old for a dancer."

She resisted the urge to cringe. What was he alluding to?

"But I'm happy to see that you used your time away from us wisely." Artum leaned forward in his seat. "Instead of being a soloist, what would you say if I were to instead promote you to principal?"

"Principal?" she sputtered. "I mean… it would be an honor. It's something that I've dreamed about since I was a little girl." Clara's mind drifted to the years of schooling and sacrifices she made.

Artum had never been so kind to her before. Usually everything was treated like a business transaction between them. Clara knew she wasn't one of the favorites, but she stayed out of the way, learned quickly, and did her job.

"Excellent. With all the attention you're about to receive, there is no question you'll bring in a whole batch of new donors. Do you think you could mention to Prince David we'd like to have him host our *Nutcracker* fundraisers? After the budget issues we had last year, your romance couldn't have come at a better time."

Her face started to burn. Many questions ran through her mind. "Excuse me? What are you talking about? Prince David?"

Artum's mouth tightened. "You don't have to play coy with me. The news broke this morning. It's all over the internet."

"What's all over the internet?"

"You dating Prince David."

Clara's crutches clattered to the ground. She fumbled for her phone. As she unsilenced it and unlocked the screen, she took note of about twenty missed calls from David, Amanda, and a few other unknown numbers.

She launched her internet browser and typed in her name. The top results yielded articles with headlines reading: "Boring Royal Might Not Be So Boring After All," "The Boring Royal Bags Ballerina," and "Leeds and His Leading Lady."

Her hand flew to her mouth. "No. No. No. No. No."

She tapped on a link halfway down the page.

The bachelor prince may not be a bachelor for much longer! A source close to the royal family reports that Prince David has secretly been dating American ballerina Clara Little for an unspecified length of time. The two have been reported as appearing all over London when Little was in town for a charity gala performance. For an exclusive look at how their romance has been unfolding and to hear about what Clara Little's fellow ballerinas had to say about her, see page three.

"I don't know why you're seeing this as such a bad thing, Clara. It's about time you do something useful for the company."

"Useful for the company?" Clara's head jerked up. Her jaw clenched. "What do you call all the extra things I've done for you and the company over the past five seasons? I've showed up to class and rehearsals *every* single day ready to dance no matter what. I've skipped out on taking *any* vacations so I could fill in on short notice for dancers who were ill or injured. I've even pushed through my own injuries because I knew the company was short on bodies. Was that not being useful to you?"

"Clara, quit being so dramatic. You were doing what was in your contract."

Her fists clenched. Was this how Artum saw her? Did she truly only hold material value to the man she'd danced for the last five years?

Suddenly, she recalled an earlier conversation she'd had with Igor. "Is the only reason you bother promoting me to soloist because Igor told you if you didn't, there was a chance another company might hire me for the position?"

Artum's face paled. "It may have come up once, but I can't remember."

All this time, I've given my loyalty to LABT, and they never even believed in me! Could I have become a principal dancer by now somewhere else?

"Did you ever see me as being more than a corps member?"

Artum scratched his forehead. "Clara, let's not do this."

She pounded her fist on his desk. "Answer me. I have to know."

"When you received a contract offer from LABT during your first season, I owed a favor to the Seattle Ballet Academy's director. Carl had talked Mitzi Fellows into joining us as a principal dancer instead of one of the New York companies. In return, he told me that he had a former student who could be useful to me since she was a quick study."

Clara's head began to throb. *Mitzi was two classes below mine. She won a million different ballet competitions. Every company wanted her because she's so tall and willowy.* Hearing the truth burned. Artum had only hired her because her old teacher had asked him to.

She'd heard enough. "I quit."

He flinched. "Clara, be reasonable. At the end of the day, ballet is a business. You can't blame me for doing what I can to stay afloat."

She retrieved her crutches from the ground. "Don't say anything else. I refuse to be used as the company's marketing tool for being tied to someone famous. I'm one of the hardest-working dancers out there. I know I'm talented. There are plenty of other companies who will see the value I bring to them with my dancing. Goodbye, Artum. I won't be seeing you again."

Clara tried hard to keep her emotions in check and was able to make it out the door before breaking down. She walked quickly to an empty stairwell, not wanting to go out in public just yet. She needed to be strong. She couldn't believe she'd just quit LABT.

Clara reached for her phone. Double checking once more that she was alone, she dialed Amanda's number.

"C! Oh. Em. Gee. About time you called! Tell me what you need from me."

This was her best friend. She didn't ask how she was doing. She jumped straight into asking how she could help.

"I just quit LABT. Can you come pick me up? I might need your evasive driving skills."

"Text me the address and I'll be there in twenty."

She wiped her puffy eyes and sniffled. "Sharing my location with you now."

"Got it. Just making a U-turn now." Clara heard the sound of a couple cars honking their horns. She imagined Amanda cutting across lanes of busy traffic.

"Thank you, A."

"That's what friends are for."

Chapter Thirty-One
DAST

♕

"**A**nd you're certain she is safe at your flat?" David questioned, pacing his study.

"I swear on my collection of *I Love Lucy* DVDs that when I parked in my complex's garage, we were totally alone. I made sure when I picked Clara up that we took the scenic detour. Trust me, none of the trashy gossip-rag photographers was able to keep up with me. I drive fast, and I happen to know LA intimately."

He let out a deep breath. "And her mental health?"

"She's exhausted and running on empty. Her entire life has just been flipped upside down. She was surprisingly calm about quitting her dream job, but it's the ferociousness of the media that's rattled her. Clara has always had a tiny online presence. Which you'd think would be good, except instead, it's made the media even hungrier to know more about her. They're paying big bucks for anyone to come forward with a story about her. It's disgusting and twisted."

And this is just the beginning. Even though we aren't together, now that she's been linked to me, they won't stop.

They'll only want more, like an ancient Greek hydra monster. Cut off one head and two more emerge.

"I wouldn't advise letting her return to her flat until we figure out the security arrangements." David pinched the bridge of his nose. "I know she's not a fan of it, but now that things are starting to get out of control, I'm afraid I'm going to have to insist she have someone with her at all times."

"She knows that." Amanda lowered her voice. "We chatted about it in the car. She has two roommates, and they said the complex was packed so full of media vans and mopeds that they had to leave their cars at LABT and order a car to drop them off."

David swallowed hard. "Do you think she'll accept a call from me when she wakes up?"

"I do."

"And what if I were to come out there… do you think she'd be willing to see me?"

"Totally. She's been miserable without you. I can't stand to watch much more of it. You two have been apart long enough. The faster you make up and get back together, the better—the faster we can skip to the happily ever after," Amanda said.

He switched his mobile phone to his other hand. "Then that settles it. I'll book myself a ticket for tomorrow."

"Please do."

"Thank you so much for chatting with me Amanda. Clare-bear is lucky to have a friend like you."

She sighed. "It works both ways. I'm lucky to have her too."

"Is there anything else you think I can do in the meantime?"

Amanda told him no. She'd take care of Clara until he

was able to see her in person. Placing his mobile down on his desk, he removed his glasses, and rubbed his eyes.

I need a distraction. Swimming's out. It's too early to make the drive to Buckingham Palace. Running, it is.

～

Half an hour later, David was let into Eddie's residence by a sleepy-looking butler. He climbed the steps to his cousin's bedroom. Eddie slept soundly, sprawled out in the middle of his sheets and blankets in a tangled mess.

"Edmund, training drill time," he yelled at the top of his lungs, then pulled his younger cousin out of bed.

"Sod off…" a sleepy Prince of Wales slurred, and tried to go back to sleep.

"Wake up. You need to be ready to train."

It's a win-win for both of us. I have someone to push me to train, and Eddie gets used to keeping early hours before he leaves for boot camp.

"Urg, I'm up." He threw a pillow at David and rolled out of his bed.

"Let's go. A run. Now."

Eddie was up and ready to go within a few minutes. He dressed in shorts and a light hoodie and was slow to tie his trainers. He met David downstairs. They walked outside and shivered in the cold, brisk morning air.

"What's happening?" Eddie asked, yawning. "You only wake me up at dawn and punish me with running if I've done something wrong or you have something on your mind."

"That's exactly what I need you for. I need to clear my head." David indicated they would run through the palace grounds.

They set out on a path near the garden. A dense layer of trees hid them from public view. Eddie grumbled under his breath. "I should pull rank here. Technically, as the Prince of Wales, you should be listening to me."

"Pulling rank. I'm impressed." David's voice oozed with sarcasm. The two took off at a steady pace for warm-up.

Eddie snorted.

David responded by picking up their pace into a steady jog.

"What did you want to discuss?"

"Clara."

"What about her?"

"The public knows about her connection to us"

Eddie groaned.

"Exactly."

Eddie started to breathe harder. "You don't think Aunt Charlotte would've hinted to the press about her, do you?"

"No. The thought did cross my mind, but Mum wouldn't sink that low. She been, er… coaching me on the art of how to be romantic."

His cousin raised an eyebrow. "How on earth is she doing that?"

"By having me conduct character studies on the male romance heroes she claims have ruined real-life romance for women."

Eddie frowned. "Er… right."

David chuckled. "You asked."

"I'm sorry I did."

"Race you to the tree." He turned their run into an all-out sprint. Eddie pulled ahead, matching him stride for stride, but David was taller and better trained. As Eddie slowed, he just pulled ahead. Hugging the base of the grand old oak tree for support, he breathed hard.

"What are you going to do about Clara and the press?" Eddie ask between wheezing breaths in and out.

"First, I'm going to apologize and try and win her back."

"I thought you'd sorted all that out."

David rested his hands on top of his head. "Not exactly."

"David." Eddie face-palmed. "Mate, why the bloody hell haven't you?"

"I wanted to give her the time and space she needed to figure out if she wants a future with me. I know what I want, but she needed to come to terms with her decision on her own. I won't force her into a relationship with me if she wants privacy. We live under a microscope. Everything we do, people are curious about." David sank back against the tree. "I love her too much to do that to her."

Eddie was his closest friend and ally—essentially David's brother. He was one of the few people he could be himself around and express his true thoughts and emotions to.

"And now that word is out about her, she's out of time," his cousin whispered.

David nodded. "I think she feels the same way as I do, but what if she doesn't? I don't know if I could handle the rejection. She's *the* one. I know she is."

"So don't give her a chance to reject you. What have the blokes you've been reading about or studying done to make their women swoon?"

"A grand gesture."

Eddie rolled his eyes. "Such as?"

David rambled off the first things that popped into his mind. "Writing letters? Serenading with a guitar? A picnic?"

"Those aren't grand. Those are average. Think bigger. Think better."

"It's not about how big a gesture is, Eddie, it's about how meaningful it is. That it comes from the heart. It's a physical way of showing love." As soon as the words were out of his mouth, an idea popped into his head. "I know what I need to do."

"Brilliant. What are you going to do?"

A ghost of a smile crossed his lips. "Wouldn't you like to know?"

"Does it involve going to California? Can I go with you? We can call it my last hurrah before I leave civilian life. Do you think we might be able to squeeze in a surfing lesson? I've always wondered about it. Or even a visit to one of the amusement parks there?"

David knelt down and tightened the laces on his trainers. "Yes it does, and yes you can... if you beat me back."

Eddie's right. I'm not going to give Clara any option but to see me and let me show her how much I care for her. I'm coming for you, Clare-bear. Your friend Amanda better watch out, because I'm bringing her a gift too.

Chapter Thirty-Two
CLARA

Ballet was Clara's sanctuary. She breathed deeply, gripping the back of a chair, slowly extending her right foot out to the side for a tendu. It was a simple movement that she'd been able to do since she was five. But now, as she worked toward rebuilding all her tiny intrinsic muscles, it felt foreign.

Her body needed to relearn the most basic steps. Some people might have found it frustrating, but Clara tried to look at it as a victory. Every plié, tendu, battement, and other basic ballet barre movement brought her one step closer to returning to the stage.

Not having a clear deadline demarking when she needed return to full strength lifted a huge weight off her shoulders. She could take the time to listen to her body, not forcing it to do more than it was capable of. *All* her injuries would have a chance to heal.

When I return, I'll be back stronger than when I left.

The muscles in the arch of her foot began to cramp. She turned the chair around and sat down, rubbing her hands over a stiff spot. The skin was soft and tender.

Today's plan: Take as many breaks as needed to get through at least dégagés and rond de jambes standing, then I can start on some floor exercises. By the time I finish, Amanda should be back, and we can have lunch together.

Picking her phone from the bedside table, Clara checked her text messages.

"Honey, I'm home!" Amanda called out from the kitchen.

"That was fast."

Amanda shrugged as she poked her head inside the doorway of the guest room Clara was using. "BBQ Shack just opened for the day." Her friend looked at her closely. "You're frowning. What's up?"

"Oh, the same as yesterday." Clara tossed her phone onto the bed and huffed. "My roommates said our complex is swarming with media. There are more people camping out today than yesterday."

"Do they need a place to go? If you don't mind, they can crash here, or I can call in a few favors from some of my coworkers at the airline."

"No, they said they're fine. Actually, I think they both secretly kind of like the attention," Clara said, rubbing the back of her neck. "They're going to pack up some of my stuff for me, and I'll take a car over to pick it from one of their boyfriends' places."

"Nope. You aren't going anywhere, C." Amanda crossed her arms. "Tell them *I'll* pick it up."

Clara stared at the ground. "I can't do that. I've already caused you enough trouble."

"It's no trouble, really. You're doing me a favor by house-sitting my place. I'm never even home that often."

"Still. I'm taking up your spare room."

"C, have you taken a good look at what's actually *in here?*"

Clara lifted her chin. She'd noticed Amanda's spare uniforms, five or six pieces of oversized rolling luggage, a stack of shoe boxes, and department store bags stacked against the wall on the far side of the room near the closet. She'd resisted the urge to see what her friend kept in there. It felt like an invasion of privacy.

"No."

As if to prove a point, Amanda walked over to the closet and opened it. The life-sized cardboard cutout of Eddie and some boxes came tumbling out. "It's all stuff that won't fit in my bedroom closet. This room is literally a dumping ground. The only reason I even have a two-bedroom place is because Mom wanted Dad to be able to crash here if he ever had a flight to pilot out of LAX, but that's *never* happened. So quit feeling guilty."

Amanda picked up some of the items off the ground and tossed them back into the closet. "If you're feeling up to it later, Mom's asked if you could call her. Just a heads-up—she's going to suggest you let her and Dad pay off the remaining portion of your lease and move in with me."

Clara blanched. "I can't do that."

"That's why I'm warning you now. If you decide to argue with Mom, you'll need to have some sort of convincing points."

Clara sighed. "Thanks for the heads-up."

Amanda held her body against the door and shoved it closed. "I forgot this was in here." She hugged the cutout of Eddie to her chest. "I'm putting you in my closet."

Eddie would die if he saw that.

"Anyway, I picked up the grilled chicken salad for you, a

bacon cheeseburger and fries for me, and a chocolate malt we can split later. Do you want to eat now, or later?"

"Now's fine. I'm at a good stopping point."

They both glanced at her swollen foot.

"Do you want me to fill the trash bin with ice so you can soak it while you eat?"

"Please and thank you."

"Oh, before I forget, this arrived for you too." Amanda disappeared for a moment, then returned with a shoebox-sizedpackage. "What did you order? It looks like it whatever it is shipped overnight from Europe."

"I didn't order anything, but let's see." She turned the package over in her hands. "Weird... there's no return address." Gently, she shook the box. It was well packed, whatever was inside. "You don't think it's hate mail or anything?"

"Doubt it. Nobody except my parents and one other person knows you're here."

Curiosity got the better of her. They moved into the living room, where the light was better and there was more space. Carefully, Clara opened the package while Amanda took the fake Eddie to her room.

"Hurry up! The anticipation is killing me, smalls," Amanda reached for the contents of the box. Clara pulled it out of her reach.

"Play nice or I won't share what's inside with you," she said playfully.

Another box was within the box, and two dust bags covered what Clara assumed to be a pair of shoes. There was no note, but inside lay a single pink ballet-flat street shoe.

Why would someone go to the trouble of sending her a single shoe? She held it up for a closer inspection. It was light and made from high-end leather. Etched into the material were delicate, intricately stitched designs of a flower, a spinning wheel, and a castle.

"It's the story of *The Sleeping Beauty*," she said.

Slipping the shoe onto her good foot, she found it fit her like a glove. She knew David had made this for her. Clara was at a loss for words.

She took the shoe off, hugged it to her chest, and cried. Her body shook as the salty tears ran down her face. She thought about just how much care and love David had put into making the shoe just for her. She could almost smell the woodsy scent of his cologne. She remembered the way his eyes crinkled at the corners when he smiled, the way his voice was a soothing melody that could calm her restless heart. She thought about how firm his arms were when they held her in a warm embrace and the way his lips brushed against hers when they'd kissed a few weeks ago.

As Clara sat there, she realized that it wasn't just longing or a sense of loss that she felt—it was a reminder that she loved David. She had been so determined to prove a point during their last argument that she had completely missed the mark of *why* he'd wanted to protect her. He loved her. And now, she realized just how deeply she cared for him. They'd both made mistakes.

She was determined to make things right. She wasn't going to waste another moment separated from him. She needed David in her life. She had to call him. Her phone was still on the bed in the other room. As she stood up from the couch to retrieve it, however, she realized that Amanda was no longer in the room. Instead, standing in the doorway, in a navy-blue suit, white dress shirt, and glasses, stood the man she'd longed to see.

"David," she whispered.

"Cheers, Clare-bear." He smiled at her.

They closed the distance between one another, and a moment later, she was in his arms again. She buried her face in his jacket. She soaked in his scent of sandalwood and cinnamon. "I've missed you so much, David. I'm sorry I was so upset with you," she said into his jacket.

"I'm sorry too. Will you accept this humble shoemaker back into your life?" David's tone was teasing.

"A thousand times yes… as long as you'll take me as I am."

"Forever and always. I love you so much."

"And I love you."

Clara's breath quickened. Her eyes met David's. She was drawn in by the crystal clarity of his blue orbs, and they leaned toward one another. Her arms reached up and encircled his neck. The shoe she'd been holding fell to the floor with a clatter.

Their lips met and they kissed with urgency. It was as if a rainstorm were pounding down upon a stretch of desert after months of hot, dry, searing heat. David ran his hands through her hair and pulled her in closer to him. When they broke apart, they both breathed heavily.

"The media has it all wrong." She walked her hands up his tie and loosened it.

"What's that?"

"They call you the boring royal, but a much better name for you would be a passionate royal."

His body shook with laughter. "Passionate, you say?"

"That's what I'm sticking to." Clara's eyelids fluttered. "But I may need some evidence before I'm fully convinced." She tugged on his tie.

"As my lady wishes." David blinked slowly, planting a slow trail of kisses on her jaw. "My beautiful, talented, sweet, darling Clare-bear."

They kissed a second time, slower and more intimate than before.

A short while later, Clara sat on the couch, mutely following his directions.

"Let's see if this fits." He knelt down on his knees and slipped the shoe onto Clara's good foot. The supple leather glided into place and fit around her hard-built calluses, like a glass slipper. "There's only one foot this was made for, and that's yours."

"I thought it took you weeks to make shoes."

"For anyone else, yes. For you though, I spent every spare moment I could working on these because I missed you. I wanted you to have a small piece of me with you."

She lifted her leg, admiring the shoe. "David, this is probably the most heartfelt thing anyone's ever done for me."

David remained kneeling and cleared his throat. From an internal pocket in his jacket, he removed the matching shoe. Holding it in front of him, he said, "Clare-bear, we may not have had the most romantic beginning together, but having spent three of the most glorious weeks with you in London, I know you are the woman who is meant to be my partner in life. I'm not asking you to marry me—yet—but I *am* offering this shoe to you as a token of my love. I promise that I will do everything in my power to be a worthy man of you, and hope that time will bring us closer to one another and deepen the love we share. What do you say? Can we start this dating thing over again?"

Clara's eyes widened. Her heart raced.

"I don't want to start over. I want us to continue building on what we have. Everything happens for a reason. Making mistakes and learning from our differences is the only way we'll be able to continue to keep growing and discovering more about one another." She licked her lips. "I love you so much, and I know that time is going to strengthen our bond. I hope you won't get sick of me, 'cause this ballerina isn't going anywhere anytime soon."

She laughed to herself.

David smiled widely. He slipped the second shoe on her other foot.

"Now hurry up and kiss me again," she said.

David didn't need to be told twice. As they kissed once more, the two remained blissfully ignorant of the world around them. Like all fairy tales, Clara had found her happily ever after.

Epilogue
CLARA

THREE MONTHS LATER

The sun was setting over the Santorini skyline, painting it in hues of pink and orange, and the water an otherworldly shade of blue. David and Clara stood on the balcony of their hotel room, soaking in the view. The air was crisp with the promise of a beautiful evening.

David took a deep breath. The ring he'd been carrying with him every day for the last two weeks burned a hole in his pocket. He tapped the lump once more to make sure it was still there.

"I'll never get tired of this view. London is beautiful at night, but this is so much grander. It's nature at its finest. Don't you agree?" Clara asked.

It was time. It was now or never to ask the most important question of his life. His heart raced, and his hands trembled as they closed around the square velvet box. Pulling it out of his pocket, he opened the lid, and took a deep breath.

"Clara," he began, his voice a gentle, heartfelt whisper. "From the moment you danced the role of Aurora, I knew that our lives would become an enchanting story of their own. We've penned our prologue, but now I'm hoping that you're ready to take the next step and write the first chapter. Together."

Clara turned to face him, her eyes shining with love and anticipation. Her hand flew to her mouth.

He continued. "You've shown me a love I never knew was possible. You've been my confidante, my strength, and my joy. You've filled my days with laughter and my nights with love. I can't imagine a future without you by my side." He knelt down on one knee. "Clara, will you do me the great honor of becoming my princess and the next Duchess of Leeds?"

Her head bobbed up and down.

Feeling as if he were literally walking on a cloud, he took the Welsh-gold and amethyst ring and slid it onto her hand.

Clara seemed overwhelmed as she teared up. "David, every moment with you has been a dream come true."

He gently cupped her face in his hands, leaning in to tenderly kiss her. Their lips met in a soft and sweet embrace, sealing their love and commitment. It was a kiss filled with promises of forever, a symbol of their journey ahead.

～

A month later, Clara and David announced to the world they were engaged.

Now, two months after that, David found himself checking the corridor and signaling to Clara that the coast was clear. As silently as a ballerina could tiptoe across the hall, she moved with the agility of a gazelle. They made an all-out sprint for Eddie's unused set of rooms and silently closed the door behind them. Both let out collective sighs of relief.

"I can't believe we've resorted to sneaking around Buckingham Palace to hide from your mother! If I hear one more question today about what type of lace I want on my wedding veil, or what type of flower I think would best represent America, I'm going to scream. I knew Princess Charlotte was going to be intense, but I never knew she'd be the type of person who would put together three entire binders solely dedicated to the different types of fabric that could be used in my wedding dress," Clara whispered as she and David finally found a spare moment of time to be alone together.

He took her hand and squeezed it. "Clare-bear, I warned you not to tell Mum we were engaged at all, but no, you had to go and set her off. We're going to be hearing about every single detail from now until next spring. You sure you wouldn't rather elope?" David joked. He let Clara rest her head on him as they sat on Eddie's bed.

She rolled her eyes at him. "If we didn't involve your mom, one, it would shatter her heart, and two, I'd never hear the end of it." Clara sighed. "At least letting her take over most of the wedding planning has given me ample time to build up my dance stamina. I think I'm finally ready to start auditioning for a new company."

Clara closed her eyes and reflected back to the whirlwind of excitement they had been through. The decision to move to London was a no-brainer after leaving LABT.

There really wasn't anything left for her in LA, except for Amanda, whose job brought her through London often enough. The move would have happened sooner rather than later. She was happily settled into David's apartment at Kensington Palace and life in the UK.

The Westminster Ballet had been extra accommodating in granting Clara access to its physical therapists and studios. In return, she'd started teaching a variation class once a week to the students of the Upper School. Mr. Williamson had hinted that anytime she was ready, she could submit an audition to join the company. He still had not hired anyone since Evelyne Murdoch's retirement.

Now that she was back in dancing shape, she hoped she could take him up on his offer. She appreciated the fact that he was putting her through the same audition process as any other dancer. She wanted to earn her spot based on her talent, even if it seemed likely he would just hand it to her.

David shook his head. "I know exactly what you're thinking, Clare-bear. Being my wife and a future royal shouldn't stand in the way of you being able to achieve your hopes and dreams. I cannot wait to see you start dancing again." He wrapped his arms around her and gently kissed the top of her head.

Clara picked at some of the loose threads of her yoga pants. "I just hope I can still have that spark when I dance on stage. It's been more than six months."

"You will. Trust me," David answered without hesitation, rubbing circles on her hand.

Clara stood and stretched. "You're right. I need to stop doubting myself. I am a good dancer. I'm principal material. I'm so much stronger physically and mentally than when I last danced."

"Brilliant, now we can discuss what to do about Amanda and Eddie." David laughed, adjusting his glasses. "I'm afraid they're going to be attached at the hip before you know it."

"Is that such a bad thing? Eddie's been doing so well with his army training. Amanda's crazy schedule and random visits to London are exactly what he needs to keep him on his toes." Clara laughed too. "Let them see where their own dating life takes them."

They enjoyed a few more moments of quiet before the door burst open. In walked Princess Charlotte. Clara groaned internally.

"There you two are! Honestly, it's like wrangling a pair of wild horses. Clara, you and I need to discuss what the invitations are going to look like. We also need to get a head start on the guest list. I have narrowed down my suggestions to about five hundred." David's mother placed a six-inch-wide binder on Eddie's unused desk.

"Actually, Charlotte, we were just about to leave for the Royal Opera House. I have something I'd like to discuss with Mr. Williamson." Clara's voice was hopeful and full of enthusiasm.

"Perfect, I have a meeting with the board of directors at two. You don't mind if I join you while you motor over?"

David and Clara quickly exchanged guilty looks.

His mother continued speaking, appearing not to take notice of it. "Clara, dear, it hasn't been announced yet, but it's been decided that the Westminster Ballet's first program of the year is going to be *The Sleeping Beauty*. I just happen to know that Mr. Williamson is on the lookout for a new principal. What a coincidence, is it not?"

Clara laughed nervously. "Yeah, it is."

Her journey had come full circle.

"Well, Mother, Clara, shall we?" David guided his two leading ladies out of the room and on to their next adventure.

The world was a smaller place than it seemed.

The Sleeping Beauty was a beast of a ballet. Let the new challenges commence.

Dear Reader

Thank you for taking the time to read "Dancing With a Royal."

If you enjoyed this book, please take a moment to leave a review on Amazon, Goodreads, Bookbub, or whatever platform you may have discovered this book on. It helps Tomi connect with readers like you!

Love her books? Become a part of her treasured community here.

Stay connected with Tomi by scanning QR code, or by visiting her official website.

Https://TomiTabb.com

DEAR READER

About the Author

Tomi's publishing journey began in 2020 with the release of her debut novel, *Dancing With a Royal*. Although she's always loved writing fictional stories, Tomi's background is in academic writing. She holds an MA degree in History and is currently pursuing her doctorate degree in the same subject.

In her rare free time, Tomi enjoys figure skating and hunting for new pumpkin flavored foods to try. It's one of the many reasons fall is her favorite season.

Tomi is a California native where she resides with her family and one very spoiled cat.

Website: TomiTabb.com

Also by Tomi Tabb

The Unexpected Royals
-Dancing With a Royal
-Jiving With a Royal
-Designing for a Royal
-More Than a Passing Shot

Friends of the Unexpected Royals
-Designs on Love
-Engineering Love

Novellas Related to the Unexpected Royals Series
-Pointe Shoes and Sugar Plums
-A Game of Small Victories

The Skaters of Sequoia Valley
-The Rules of the Rink
-The Sloth Zone

The Royals of Isola Nostrum
-The Great Austen Adventure
-For the Love of Dinosaurs

Historical Romance
-The Mysterious Mr. Marcellus

Made in the USA
Columbia, SC
03 May 2025